ICED SPY

——

a Bison Creek Mystery

A. GARDNER

CHAPTER ONE

I couldn't explain what I saw when I opened the door to my tiny apartment over the Painted Deer Bookshop. All I could think was, *why?* Why was my sister jumping up and down like the scratches on my couch were a good thing? *She's finally snapped.*

"Joy?" I said out loud, shutting the door behind me and sidestepping my way to the kitchen to keep the mud on my boots from spreading into the living room. My car had died just up the street. Again. "What's going on?" I shook off the gust of snow flurries that had followed me inside. Bison Creek was on the brink of another snowstorm. One that was sure to bring in a murderous freeze.

"Don't freak out, Essie." Joy bit the corner of her lip and, as was her habit, rubbed her forearm—a portion of her skin covered entirely by tattoos. "He won't be here long. I promise."

"*He?*" I glanced down at our furry visitor. A black and white cocker spaniel walked forward to smell my shoe. His long, floppy ears bounced as he looked up at me with his giant puppy dog eyes. I couldn't deny he was cute, but all I could think about as I stared at his eager peepers was the mess of poo I would most likely have to clean up.

"Yes," Joy replied. She took a deep breath and brushed a strand of hair over her shoulder. It was the same shade of espresso as mine. "Essie, I'd like you to meet my new baby. Well…dog. His name is Miso."

"Miso? Like the soup?"

"Yep," a voice chimed in from Joy's bedroom. Wade emerged, wearing nothing but boxer shorts, which was an improvement from yesterday's *au naturel*. Wade was just as opinionated as my sister, and together the pair of them was a deadly combo. Wade ran his fingers through his shoulder-length locks that were normally pulled back in a ponytail. "Your sister's a mama now. Of course, I wanted to name him something more manly...like Cam."

"We're not naming our dog after your Camaro," Joy said through her teeth, the joyous grin momentarily wiped from her face.

"Sorry, babe." Wade took back his comment the moment he saw Joy's cheeks turn scarlet.

"Right," I responded. "Uh, Joy, can I see you in my room for a second?" I tilted my head away from Joy's ex-husband, ex-boyfriend, and new lover or whatever he was now. Their relationship was beyond complicated.

"Oh, but—"

"*Now.*" I slid my jaw forward, giving her the same look our mom made when we used to sneak designer heels from her closet. Joy followed me immediately, along with her new furry playmate. As soon as the two of them entered my bedroom, I shut the door.

"Calm down," Joy said. "It's just a dog."

"Isn't that what you said to Mom and Dad back in high school? But as I recall the little critter in question was a calico you found behind the bleachers." I paused and waited for her to think through her next response. Joy's eyes darted from me to the window.

She obviously didn't understand what I was referring to, but I'd spent an entire summer cleaning cat poop out from under the dryer while she was off with Wade. "This is where you promise me that you'll look after him."

"Of course I'm going to look after him." She folded her arms and narrowed her eyes like it was a stupid thing for me to say. "That's the whole reason Wade and I adopted him. I need to tap into my maternal side."

"Why?" I studied her up and down. Now that Joy was the new official Head Event Coordinator at the Pinecliffe Mountain Resort, I saw her even less. Sometimes she stayed over at Wade's and sometimes she slept at the hotel so she could get more work done. I eyed her lower abdomen. No extra bulge. No bags underneath her eyes that suggested she was sick or sleep-deprived.

"Because," Joy answered. She cleared her throat, watching Miso sniff the perimeter of my bedroom. "Wade and I have decided to move in together." Her eyes stayed glued on my expression, but the look on my face didn't change. I'd heard this all before. The first time was right before her and Wade's wedding. Though after they'd officially divorced, all I heard was what a mistake that had been. "What is it? Aren't you happy for me?"

"Yes, but—"

"Come on," she butted in. "Things are different this time. Wade and I are older and more mature. I think I'm ready to give it another go."

"Wade," I repeated. "More *mature*?"

"Okay, so that man needs a lot of work," she admitted with a chuckle.

"Well, he's got boxers on. That's a start."

"I bought those for him," Joy replied. "Besides, now you'll have the whole apartment to yourself. That's a good thing, isn't it? Didn't Patrick just get home from the hospital?" She raised her eyebrows. The mention of Patrick made my stomach churn.

"He hasn't called me yet." Every night I replayed our last conversation in my head. The two of us had agreed to a fresh start. A do-over once he recovered, beginning with a harmless coffee date.

"He will," Joy insisted. "Just don't put your eggs all in one basket, okay? You're a catch whether Patrick calls or not."

"I know," I blurted out. "I'm perfectly content with the way my life is going. I'm a fit, single woman in my early thirties, and I'm not that shy, overweight teenager I once was." I lifted my chin with confidence. A clever facade that kept Joy from reminding me of all the times I'd spent crying because of Patrick. It wasn't until I went away to college that I'd truly stopped thinking about my long-time childhood crush.

Until about a month ago when he'd moved back to Bison Creek.

I guess if Joy could forgive my rocky past with Patrick, I could forgive her neurotic adventures with her ex-husband.

"Glad to hear it." Joy nodded, glancing down at Miso. "So, you're okay with all of this?"

"I figured it was coming," I admitted. "And you and Wade haven't tried to murder each other yet so...."

"Phew." Joy sighed as she plopped herself down on my bed. "I was worried for a second that you'd have a hissy fit about having to pay full rent."

"Oh." *I didn't think of that.*

"You will be able to cover it, right?"

"I'll talk to Mrs. Tankle about it," I replied. My stomach churned even more. I had some money saved up, but now I needed that to fix my car. Or, more realistically, buy a new one.

"You could always get a new roommate," she joked. "Maybe Patrick is interested." She reached down to scratch Miso behind his ears. "Isn't that right, Miso baby?" The tone of her voice changed when she talked to Miso. It went up an octave, and she looked at him wide-eyed the same way she did when she spotted smiling babies at the corner market.

"Funny."

"Look," Joy began, "I know you just got home from work, but I'm in a real bind. I need to get some work done at the resort tonight. The Sugar Mountain Bake-Off is next weekend, and if I don't get it right Mr. Kentworth will have my head."

"Yes, I know. The entire town won't shut up about it." Sugar Mountain was a company that sold baking supplies, and every year they hosted a bake-off for a cash prize. The winning recipe would also be featured on the Sugar Mountain website.

"Yep," Joy continued. "Mr. Kentworth is really pushing Aggie and the entire kitchen staff to come up with something ground-breaking. Like the hotel doesn't have enough press to deal with already." After Lila Clemton, the beloved *and psychotic* model turned actress, was spotted here last month, tourists had been arriving by the bus loads. The Pinecliffe Mountain Resort was completely booked, and it was becoming harder and harder to secure a good parking spot on Canyon Street. Though if a routine jump-start couldn't revive my car, the lack of parking wouldn't matter to me anymore.

"Let me guess," I responded. "You need a babysitter."

"Please, Essie. Just this once."

I rolled my eyes.

"Why can't Wade watch him?" I asked.

"It's guys' night at the Grizzly." Joy jumped to her feet, clasping her hands in front of her. "Please, you owe me one—"

"If you bring up the ice cave incident again I think I might slap you." The ice cave story was her crutch for guilting me into favors. It'd been a harmless trip when we were kids that turned deadly when I'd slipped and almost fell into a darkened pit with who-knows-what waiting for me at the bottom. Joy had grabbed my hand at the last minute.

"Fine." She paused. "But just remember that you might be dead right now if it wasn't for me."

"I might be dead right now if it wasn't for *me*," I replied, reflecting back to the events of last month when I'd had a gun pointed at my face. And that was after the same culprit had tried to crush my skull with a weight from the gym.

"I've got to get going." Joy checked her watch and scrambled back into the living room searching for her shoes.

"Joy—"

"I have a late dinner meeting," she shouted from her bedroom. The sound of Miso's paws echoed on the hardwood floors as he followed her around the apartment wagging his tail. "Where's my coat?"

"Kitchen table." I waited for her to re-emerge. She nodded when she saw her usual winter coat hanging from a kitchen chair. Joy treated our common space like her own personal closet.

"I'm off, babe." Wade stepped out of Joy's room wearing faded jeans and a light jacket. He was so used to the cold that it didn't seem to bother him much. In fact, he'd walk down the street stark naked if the law permitted. "See you, Essie."

"Wade—"

Before I could ask him why he couldn't bring Miso with him to the bar, he slammed the front door. Joy dug through her handbag, making sure she had everything before shooting me a quick wave on her way out.

"Bye," I said out loud.

Miso sat near the door for a few minutes before joining me in the kitchen for a pre-dinner snack. I tried to stick with fruit, granola, or one of my homemade protein bars. The last batch I made was gobbled down in one sitting by Wade, who claimed they looked too much like brownies. I grabbed an apple from the fruit basket on the table, glancing at Miso as I took my first bite. Miso didn't wait long to beg for a piece.

"So I guess it's just you and me," I sighed. "I'm sorry, but I don't know much about dogs." I scanned the apartment from where I was sitting. "Did my sister even buy you food? A dog bed? Chew toys, maybe?" All I could spot was the leash hanging from the coat rack near the front door. It matched the olive green collar around Miso's neck. "Do you want to go for a walk? What am I saying? It's freezing outside."

Miso barked lightly at my comment and trotted to his leash.

"Do you have to go potty?" I said. I took a minute to assess the words that came out of my mouth. Just like Joy, I was already talking to Miso like he was a two-year-old. It must be the glossy puppy dog eyes.

I took another few bites of my apple and stood up to put my snow boots back on. Miso waited patiently for me to zip up my coat and lead him outside. Snow flurries rested on his curly coat as we walked down a flight of stairs and past the front of the bookshop belonging to Mrs. Tankle, avid quilter and also my nosy landlady. The door to her bookshop chimed as she flung it open.

"Oh, Essie, dear," Mrs. Tankle shouted. She attempted to follow me down the icy sidewalk in her house slippers. Even though she owned a house in town, Mrs. Tankle treated her shop like it was her sole residence. She was in every morning before breakfast, and had frequent visitors over for tea during business hours.

"Yes, Mrs. Tankle?"

"I wanted to let you know I got a new shipment of cookbooks in." She smiled, eyeing the ball of fur on the other end of my leash. Miso tried to yank me forward, but I didn't oblige. "I think I have one you might be interested in. It has lots of vegetables on the cover."

"Thanks." I pressed my lips together to keep myself from giggling. Whether it was a handwritten copy of her latest sugar-free apple pie recipe or a clipping from a magazine on heart disease, Mrs. Tankle always found a reason to stop me on the street. I'd lived above her shop for so long that she was basically my adopted grandmother.

"Whose dog?" she asked.

"Oh…" I stalled for time, kicking a pile of snow with my boots as Miso attempted to yank me away.

"Now, Essie, you know the rules. I've got to approve of any animal you keep upstairs. Poor old Bing just had kittens and I can't have them ravaged by some wild animal." *Leave it to Mrs. Tankle to name her new cat after a cherry.*

"He's not a wolfhound," I replied. "Miso is a harmless spaniel that my sister adopted."

"Essie—"

"He won't be upstairs for long, Mrs. Tankle. I promise."

Miso yanked at his leash again, but this time he did it harder. He pressed his nose to the ground and started forward, letting out a loud bark that startled Mrs. Tankle.

"If he barks like that during the day it could disrupt my customers," she mentioned.

"He won't," I assured her.

Miso paused and looked at me, his nose wet with melted snowflakes. He yanked at his leash again but this time he'd waited for an opportune moment. His leash slipped from my grasp, leaving him free to race down Canyon Street toward the Pinecliffe Mountain Resort.

I hardly blinked before I raced after him. My heart pounded, and my lungs felt like glaciers in my chest. The frozen air made it even harder to breathe, but I tried to ignore it. Joy would kill me if I lost her new pup on the very day she'd brought him home.

I ran down Canyon Street, Bison Creek's tourist-friendly main street, and chased Miso closer to the hotel near Pinecliffe Mountain. Miso stopped at the bridge at the end of the road. The bridge linked the old part of town with the newer half—the half where out-of-towners usually bought their vacation homes. It was also a passageway over the creek that joined with Lake Loxley. I surveyed the bridge and its edges that were overridden with icicles. The aspens along the creek were dusted with winter powder, and the ground looked just as snowy.

"Miso!" I shouted.

Miso sniffed the ground some more, staying close to the icy riverbank until it met the frozen shore of Lake Loxley. The lake was covered in sheets of ice, with thick ice around the edges and thin, cracked ice in the center. The water underneath was so cold it would probably give me frostbite if I so much as dipped the tip of my finger in it. *Please, don't fall in.*

I took every step with caution, grateful when Miso came to a halt in the distance. His midnight coat was easy to spot against the white snow. Miso nudged at something on the shore. Something that at first looked like a pile of iced-over rocks dusted with frost, until I got closer.

"What the…?" A surge of adrenaline pulsed through my veins, making my thick coat feel much too warm. A bead of sweat trickled down my forehead, and my eyes went so wide I had to scrape the flurries from my eyelashes. Miso glanced up at me, waiting for his next command. But he had done plenty already. I reached down and checked for a pulse.

Nothing.

Time to call the sheriff.

Miso had found a dead body.

CHAPTER TWO

The body next to Lake Loxley looked like a block of ice. A fresh layer of snow hid most of it, apart from the spots Miso had uncovered. I'd pulled out my cell phone and called the sheriff as soon as Miso started sniffing the victim's shoes. I nudged him away from the body, but Miso focused on nothing other than brushing the snow away with his paws.

The body was lying face down, but I knew all too well who it was. *Sunflower yellow.* It was a client of mine named Sarah Henson. A woman I'd only trained a handful of times, but I saw her almost every morning on my way to work. She'd be up sometimes even before the bakery opened its doors walking her two Akitas—large dogs with bear-like heads and coats that were colored white and sandy brown. Sarah Henson always wore a similar outfit when she went out walking. Her sunflower yellow ski jacket had been a hard thing to miss.

"Miso," I scolded him, glancing up and down the shoreline for any signs of a struggle. Miso continued brushing the snow from the victim's legs. My eyes darted to the rocks and chunks of ice around the body. No footprints. No paw prints. And no leash. I'd never seen Sarah Henson out walking without her two dogs.

When Miso reached the back of Sarah Henson's head, he stopped and let out a sudden bark. A crimson stain had seeped through her tangled hair and turned the snowflakes around it scarlet. I took a deep breath. This wasn't the first time I'd found a body. My mind automatically jumped to the worst conclusion—the conclusion that was confirmed when I'd found a dead bridesmaid at the Pinecliffe Mountain Resort spa last month.

Murder.

"Hey!" The sheriff and his son, Murray, had arrived. They were the father-son duo who made up the Bison Creek sheriff's department, though I'd heard rumors that their numbers would be growing soon due to the recent influx of tourists.

"Murray, over here!" I shouted back, tightening my grip on Miso's leash. Murray walked slowly toward me. His reddish hair was parted to the side as usual, and the way he grinned only emphasized the way his front teeth stuck out.

"Well, what do we have here?"

"Sarah Henson," I replied, hanging my head.

"Actually, I meant the dog," Murray joked.

"Show some respect, will you?" I frowned.

"Yeah, sorry, Essie." Murray turned around and waved at his father.

Sheriff Ronald Williams was a sturdy old man, and he moved at the pace of an elderly snail. Unless there was an arrest to be made. I'd seen him wrestle a grown man to the floor like it had been the simplest task in the world. That's when I came up with the theory that Sheriff Williams actually wasn't a slow old man who smoked more than a pack a day. He was just in the habit of *conserving* his energy. Sheriff Williams stroked his gray mustache and scratched at a scab on the side of his hand.

"Dang thing," he muttered, picking at the scab. "That's the last time I volunteer to peel the potatoes."

"You know that cut would heal a lot faster if you didn't smoke like a steam engine," I greeted him.

"Good to see you, Essie." Sheriff Williams and I had our differences, but after the madness that went down last month on the slopes of Pinecliffe Mountain, we had a mutual understanding. *Mainly, no name-calling.*

My heart raced as I spotted a third man not far behind him. A man who wasn't dressed like the others. A man who had stopped to observe the icicles on the bridge and my footprints in the snow. He limped slightly as he continued walking, favoring his right knee.

"Who is that?" I lowered my voice, attempting to get a good look at his face. "Is he from around here?"

"He only responds to Detective Keene," Murray whispered. "Trust me, don't call him Cydney."

"Thanks for the tip."

"How far would you say we are from Canyon Street?" Detective Keene chimed in from afar, barely even acknowledging me.

"Not very," Murray answered him.

"I meant in yards, *Officer*." Detective Keene was much more direct than his colleagues. His dark hair was trimmed short and gelled so that it sparkled under the sunlight. Not a wrinkle was in sight on his dark slacks, and unlike Murray's, his shirt was tucked in.

"Oh." Murray rubbed the side of his wrinkled pant leg. "That makes more sense."

Detective Keene made a few more observations of the surrounding area, and even snapped a few photos. Next, he moved on to the body. His eyes ran over it thoroughly, starting with the tips of Sarah Henson's snow boots.

"Ahem." Detective Keene glared down at Miso, who was standing in his way. I carefully tugged at Miso's leash.

"Detective Keene," Sheriff Williams said, pointing to me, "this is Essie Stratter, one of our locals." Cydney Keene paused to look me up and down like I was just another rock or tree.

"I see," he responded. "Do you know this woman?" I took a step forward, getting a closer look at the dark coffee color of his eyes. They matched the color of his hair. Smooth skin. Clean-shaven. Detective Keene couldn't have been much older than me, and yet he was acting as if he was running the show. What surprised me even more was that Sheriff Williams was letting him.

"That's Mrs. Henson," I answered.

"First name?"

"Sarah," the sheriff clarified.

"And I take it she's married?" Detective Keene continued.

"Widowed." The sheriff clasped his hands in front of him. "Sarah moved to Bison Creek about ten years ago, give or take a few. She married fairly quickly but her husband, Charlie, died in an avalanche a year later." Rather than extend any sympathies, Detective Keene moved on with his questioning.

"Middle-aged?"

"Yes," Sheriff Williams confirmed.

"Well," Detective Keene concluded, "a middle-aged woman who lives alone out for a walk next to an icy lake. She must've tripped."

"You can't be serious—" Before I could enlighten Cydney on what *I'd* observed, Sheriff Williams pulled me aside.

"Get Doc Henry over here," the sheriff instructed his son. "And Murray, you little cuss, don't touch anything."

Miso sniffed Sheriff Williams before deciding he didn't want to take a walk with him. Miso tried to yank me in the opposite direction as I followed the sheriff toward a nearby aspen that was far enough away to have a private conversation. I could still hear Murray and Detective Keene talking in the distance, especially when he scolded Murray for chucking rocks at the icy surface of Lake Loxley.

"What's going on here?" I whispered. "Why are you letting that *kid* walk all over you? You are still Sheriff Williams, aren't you? The guy who once wrestled a black bear back in the seventies?"

"It was Murray who spread those stories around town. He likes to run his mouth." Sheriff Williams grinned as he stroked his gray mustache. "Essie, I want to talk to you about something."

"Does it involve minding my own business?" I guessed, remembering the last time I'd tried to help him out. Sheriff Williams hadn't been very friendly with me at first.

"No. The opposite."

"What?" I glanced back at Detective Keene, who was waiting impatiently for Doc Henry to show up. The doctor's office was located on Canyon Street like most of the businesses in town, and it was only a short walk away from the crime scene.

"After what happened up at the resort last month, the mayor and the county commission have been pressuring me to hire more officers." He tilted his head. "Something about sloppy paperwork and the reassurance that this town would never see a repeat of that horrible day." What the sheriff meant to say was, he screwed up his last murder investigation, and he was on thin ice.

"You mean you weren't prepared last time," I added.

"Let's not get *too* judgmental," he immediately responded. The sheriff had a hard time admitting when he was wrong. Like the time he accused Stella Binsby, owner of the corner market, of shoplifting a loaf of cinnamon swirl from the Bison Creek Bakery. Turned out it had been a parcel of friendship bread given to her by Mrs. Adley. That particular piece of gossip circled around town for a solid month.

"Is that why *Detective Stickler* is here? To keep you all in line?"

"He's a distant relative of the mayor," the sheriff admitted, clenching his jaw. "My hands are tied on this one, Essie. That's why I need your expertise. The townsfolk trust you, and you know more about what goes on around here than this detective fellow ever will. I want you to be my eyes and ears outside the station."

"Free labor? Why would I agree to something like that?"

"The budget is tight but—"

"Hey!" Detective Keene shouted loud enough to interrupt us. "Over here!" He waved at another person who was walking leisurely toward the lake.

"That'll be the doc," Sheriff Williams muttered.

"Right over here, sir," Detective Keene said as the town doctor approached him. "I think this woman tripped and fell."

My blood boiled as I watched Detective Cydney Keene raise his chest proudly like he'd solved a decade-old mystery. Sarah Henson didn't trip and fall, and she couldn't have been out for an innocent walk. Detective Keene didn't know the people in this town like I did. Also, if he had only used his eyes he would've seen that the bloodied wound was on the *back* of her head, not the front. Which meant that she would have had to fall backwards, and then roll over somehow. Not likely, since I didn't spot any blood anywhere else near the body.

"Excuse me." I approached Detective Keene, getting his attention the best way I knew how. I let Miso sniff around the body again.

"Miss, you can't—"

"What makes you so sure that Sarah Henson tripped and fell?" I asked him. Cydney raised his eyebrows, glaring at me like he had Murray.

"I have a trained eye," the detective answered. "Now if you'll excuse me—"

"And what makes you so sure that no one else was around when she died?" I went on.

"No footprints." He nodded, straightening the collar of his jacket—brown leather, worn open to expose his badge.

"It's snowing, and why would anyone go for a breath of fresh air over here when there are plenty of safer trails around Canyon Street?" I placed my hands on my hips. Miso glanced from me to Detective Keene.

"Maybe she felt a bit daring."

"She wasn't on a walk." I raised my voice so that both the doctor and the sheriff could hear me. "Sarah Henson was murdered. I don't know why, but she was."

"Do you always jump to silly conclusions?" Detective Keene fired back.

"Only when they're right." I glanced down at the body as the town doctor, dubbed Doc Henry by Booney from the *BC Gazette* when he'd first arrived decades ago, examined Sarah Henson's head wound. "My guess is that she was running from someone."

"Essie, is it?" the detective replied, taking a step closer. "Why don't you go rattle off your *guesses* elsewhere?"

My cheeks were so warm that I could barely feel the cold. The muscles in my arms flexed, and Miso stepped between the two of us, looking as if he was ready to bare his teeth.

"No dogs," I pointed out.

"Huh?"

"Sarah Henson has two Akitas. She never goes out walking without them."

Detective Keene paused and surveyed the area again. He pulled out his notebook and jotted a few things down.

"They could've run off," he concluded. *His ego is even bigger than the sheriff's.*

"I don't see any signs that they were ever with her." I took a calming breath. "Hey, Doc, you see any poop bags in her coat pocket? Any dog treats?" Doc Henry, the only MD in town, who also moonlighted as the town coroner, assessed the rest of the body and shook his head. His white hair blended in with the frost on the trees. "Aren't Akitas known for their loyalty? I find it hard to believe that their owner dropped dead and they just ran off."

Detective Keene ground his teeth, most likely holding back comments that weren't appropriate to utter out loud.

"Perhaps we'd better swing by her house and see if her dogs are missing?" Sheriff Williams attempted to step in and play peacemaker. The role actually suited him.

"Yes, Sheriff. Maybe *we* should." Detective Keene bit the side of his lip and turned his attention toward Doc Henry. Miso let out a low growl. It was enough to bring a slight smile to my face.

"We're looking for a heavy object," the doctor announced, turning Mrs. Henson's head to the side. "Most likely circular judging from the shape of her wound."

"A rock?" Murray suggested, scratching his head.

"I don't think so," the doctor replied, scanning Lake Loxley for nearby rocks that were large enough to use as weapons. "Not unless you stumble across a rock that is about six inches in diameter and perfectly symmetrical." He chuckled to himself. "All speculation, of course."

"I'll start looking." Murray eagerly bent down to start to his search.

Sheriff Williams rubbed his forehead.

"See, Essie," the sheriff muttered. "I need all the help I can get."

"Wait a second, Sheriff." Detective Keene wrinkled his forehead when he looked at me. "The town consultant you were talking about hiring—your go-to source for the latest gossip. You didn't mean *her*, did you?"

"Can you pay me for my time, Sheriff?" I responded, ignoring Cydney's snide remark.

"I can't offer much, especially after we fill the station with more officers." Sheriff Williams shrugged.

The smirk on Detective Keene's face slowly faded as he realized that *I* was the one Sheriff Williams had spoken to him about. I pressed my lips together to stop myself from giggling. Whatever the sheriff could pay me was better than nothing, and I needed the cash to fix my car. Not to mention Joy's half of the rent when she eventually moved out.

"I'll do it." I accepted his offer with a brisk handshake. "Let's hope the killer doesn't try to shoot me this time."

CHAPTER THREE

A perk of dog-sitting Miso was that he had the uncanny ability to make everyone smile.

Even people like Mim Duvall, owner of Bone Appétit Pet Grooming, who scowled at the non-pet owners of Bison Creek. Myself included, until I strolled into her shop on Canyon Street before my first training appointment at the Pinecliffe Mountain Resort's private fitness studio.

"Oh, what a little sweetheart. Is your mommy brushing you daily, and taking you for morning walks?" Mim said hello to Miso first, bending down to rub the black and white curls on his mane. She ran her fingers over his paws and checked the inside of his mouth. Mim was the sort of woman who greeted animals as if they were people, and barked at humans as if they were animals.

"Oh, he's not mine," I clarified. "He belongs to my sister. I'm just watching him for the time being. That's why I'm here actually."

"Your mommy doesn't know what she's doing, does she?" Mim pulled a dog treat from her pocket and offered it to Miso. She had long, stringy hair that frizzed around her face and her cheeks were crowded with freckles. Jeans and a T-shirt paired with some sort of colorful vest seemed to be her cup of tea. I think she collected vests the same way I did sports bras and workout shoes.

"Do you have a pamphlet or something on Dog Care 101? The Internet seems to have mixed information on the subject." I paused as a short and stout man with bronzed skin came to the front of the store carrying boxes of supplies.

"Tell your mommy that you need a consistent schedule, daily walks and brushing, and toys to keep you busy. And if you were adopted you need to take a trip to Silverwood to visit the veterinarian." Mim didn't look up. I took a deep breath, realizing I was going to have to be more direct with her.

"Get down on all fours," the man commented. "Then she'll talk to you."

Mim glanced up at him and rolled her eyes as she slowly stood up, bringing herself back to the same level as us humans.

"This is Chip, my new assistant," Mim introduced the man with golden bronze skin.

"Actually my name's Graham, but folks just call me Chip," he clarified, tugging on his bottom lip so that the large chip in his front tooth was obvious.

"He has a rather different philosophy when it comes to dogs, but we don't judge him for it," Mim went on. "He has more experience with animals than anyone else in this town."

"I'm also *part owner* now of this little establishment. Mim always forgets that little detail. If it weren't for me, Bone Appétit might've gone under." Chip reached out and shook my hand. My eyes darted to a patch of discoloration near his elbow. A very small spot. I subtly compared the color of his arms to the color of his face. Different degrees of bronze. *Fake tanner.* "I believe that dogs should be treated as dogs, not furry little babies. After all, a dog without a pack leader is prone to misbehave."

"Oh, poppycock." Mim waved a hand, bending down again to hug Miso as he wagged his tail. "Spaniels are extra cuddly. They need lots of love and attention."

"Yeah, until they snap at you." Chip chuckled.

"He would *never* do such a thing, would you, darling?" Mim directed her comment to Miso rather than to the other humans in the room.

"Can *I* help you with something?" Chip intervened.

It was refreshing to be spoken to directly.

"Yes, thanks." I took a step closer to him, observing the whites of his eyes, which were light yellow, and...lumpy. "My sister just adopted this dog, and she has no idea how to take care of him."

"We've got a few handouts you can read." Chip searched behind the reception counter and put together a folder of papers. "Just the basics of owning a dog, but it should be enough to get you started."

As he handed me the information, I couldn't help but take a second look at the way the surface of his eyes looked like rolling hills.

"It's an eye condition," Chip pointed out.

"Sorry, I don't mean to be rude."

"Some people notice it, and some people like Mim here *don't*." He paused and glimpsed at his business partner, who was busy teaching Miso how to sit on command. "The doctors say that the lumps won't interfere with my vision. They don't bother me."

"Oh, you've been to see Doc Henry?"

"No, actually, I'm from Silverwood," he replied. "Don't judge. I come in peace."

The two of us chuckled. Silverwood was practically next door to Bison Creek, but the two cities had been rivals ever since the silver rush back in the day. Some feud between the towns' founders had since been forgotten, but the surly attitudes were still alive. The mayor of Silverwood even went as far as disallowing Patrick to practice for the X Games on Purgatory Slope, a peak that was partially within Silverwood's boundaries.

"Don't mention that if you ever head down to the Grizzly for a pint," I said.

"They'd refuse to serve me?" Chip guessed.

"Oh, they'd serve you, all right." I tucked a strand of hair behind my ear, whipping aside my long ponytail. "But if it's beer…or something else, I couldn't tell you."

"Good advice." Chip nodded. "Is there anything else I can do for you? Does your pup need a trim? I'd say he's old enough for the classic spaniel cut."

"He needs it," Mim chimed in. "The rear of his coat is completely uneven, like some amateur took scissors to it and tried to cut it. Where did you say this dog came from again?" Mim narrowed her eyes when she looked at me, making me feel like some sort of dog thief.

"I'm not sure," I answered. "Like I said, my sister brought him home."

"We'll fix him up for you." Chip snagged Miso's leash. "If you have any errands to run around town, go do that. We'll be done before you know it."

I did have one.

While I waited for Miso to finish his first appointment at Bone Appétit Pet Grooming, I pulled up to a house just outside of town. It was a two-story, well-kept Victorian with empty flower pots out front and a pair of dog bowls on the porch labeled *Carob* and *Cayenne*.

I'd never been inside of Sarah Henson's house, but I knew where she lived. She was a friend of Martha Millbreck's, the mayor's wife. I often saw Martha's car parked out front. That is, when Martha wasn't sneaking off to the next county to meet with her secret lover. I'd found out about her affair not too long ago, and Martha had managed to keep that little detail of her life a secret amidst the latest media frenzy.

I approached the front door of Sarah Henson's house and knocked. I paused, assuming I'd hear the loud barks of her two Akitas. Silence. I rang the doorbell and listened carefully. More silence. *Don't tell me Detective Know-It-All was right.*

I checked the time, knowing that if I couldn't locate Sarah Henson's dogs, I'd be forced to pursue Detective Keene's theory that Sarah had tripped and fallen and her dogs had run off in the process. I cautiously walked across the porch and tried peering through the front window. The blinds were closed and the window was locked tight. I ran my fingers across the glass and looked up at the azure sky. Like most this time of year, it was a chilly morning. Not a storm cloud was in sight, and I could clearly see the slopes on Pinecliffe Mountain that wound down to the edge of town. Compared to the cloudy grayness of yesterday when Sarah's body was found, today almost felt like a new beginning.

I trudged through the snow and toward the backyard, hoping to find at least one window that would give me a glimpse into Sarah Henson's residence. I rubbed my hands together to keep them warm, my chest beating at the same rhythm as my feet. When I reached the backyard my eye wandered to another row of empty flower pots lined up against the back of the house. One was broken.

As I moved closer, stepping over a patch of wild columbines, my chest felt like it was being immersed in Lake Loxley. My eyes went wide, focusing on the gaping hole in Sarah Henson's back window. More specifically, a section of broken glass large enough to fit a person.

I brushed a fresh coat of powder off the windowsill and glanced inside. The dining room was dark, and a harsh breeze blew past me, making the curtains flutter. I gulped, scanning the backyard one last time before carefully climbing through the window.

Even though it was light outside, the ambience in Sarah Henson's house was unmistakably dark. The dining room was drafty and plain. A simple dining room table, a few bookshelves, olive green walls. The dark stain of the wooden furniture matched the floors, making the room feel more like a gloomy cave than a lively eating area.

"Hello?" I shouted as loud as I could up the dim staircase.

I didn't want any surprises.

The living room and front foyer matched the front of the house. Dark and uninviting. I rubbed the sides of my coat and studied every detail of the bottom level right down to the wine glasses hanging next to the sink. Nothing seemed out of place. Nothing was broken, with the exception of the back window.

I inched toward the staircase and almost slipped in a clear puddle. I knelt down to take a closer look. Water…or maybe melted snow. Whoever broke in might've done so not too long ago. Droplets of water were scattered up the staircase as I headed for the second story. A small puddle met me in the hallway, and I followed it toward the master bedroom.

My heart pounded as I poked my head past the door.

Please. No more surprises.

Sarah's bed was made with a fluffy white comforter. Two white lampshades were perched on each nightstand, and half the clothes in her closet were strewn on the floor. I took a deep breath and walked toward the window. It faced the backyard and the jagged edges of the Rocky Mountains. An armchair the same shade of olive as the walls downstairs sat facing the bed, and next to it was a portrait of two white and sandy brown Akitas. I smiled, staring at the shiny gold frame that outlined the images of what were Sarah Henson's two most prized possessions.

"At least one room in this house doesn't make my skin crawl," I said out loud. In fact, Sarah Henson's bedroom did the opposite. It made me forget that I was on the trail of a murderer. I kept smiling.

Sarah's bedroom was warm and welcoming, much like the sunflower yellow ski jacket she always wore. There was a towel draped above the tub in the bathroom, and her toothbrush was next to the sink as if she'd just used it. I studied the clothes on the floor. Her walk-in closet extended farther than I'd estimated at first glance. An entire rack was bare. It was impossible to know which clothes on the floor belonged where, or if anything had been taken.

The muscles in my torso flexed as the reason for the mess of clothes finally revealed itself. Behind the empty rack in the closet was a tall safe. It sat against the closet wall, exposed like a nude feline. I tried the handle. It was locked. I pulled out my phone to call the sheriff, noticing that the rest of Sarah Henson's wardrobe hadn't been touched. More notably, all her winter coats were perfectly in place, as if they'd been made to look that way.

I raised my eyebrows, delaying my call to the station just a few minutes longer. I pushed back the section of thick winter coats that remained on their hangers, and found a hidden bookshelf. Each book was equal in size, but all were varying shades of blue, brown, and burgundy. One book in particular protruded more than the rest, though only slightly. I carefully grabbed the book and flipped through its pages, expecting to see heaps of the sort of information I might find in an encyclopedia.

But the collection of hardbacks I had found weren't books at all.

They were journals.

I raised my eyebrows, wondering if the intimate writings of a widowed dog-lover had been enough to kill for. *Doubt it.* I flipped through a few more pages and noticed that some were missing. I studied Sarah Henson's handwriting as I dialed the sheriff and listened as the phone rang.

I glanced at a sentence, rereading it a couple of times to make sure I was seeing straight.

Oh, no.

"Hello," Murray answered. "Sheriff's office."

"It's Essie," I responded quietly. I was wrong. The book in my hand wasn't what I'd thought it was. The contents gave me chills. I instinctively glanced over my shoulder, expecting to see the ghost of Sarah Henson warning me to stay away.

"Oh, Essie." Murray cleared his throat. "How's it going?"

"Murray, is your dad in?"

"You might want to hold off talking to him until he's had his morning cup of joe."

"I don't care," I replied. "Tell him to meet me at Sarah Henson's house. *Now*."

"You found her dogs?" Murray guessed.

"No." I wished that was all I'd found. "I found Pandora's box."

And I'd accidentally opened it.

CHAPTER FOUR

"I've got a safecracker coming down this weekend." Sheriff Williams sipped his morning coffee. His eyes were fixated on the pack of cigarettes in his front shirt pocket. His pinky finger tapped on his mug.

"I've got to go," I responded. "I'll keep asking around about Sarah Henson's dogs, and I'll call you later."

"Yeah." Sheriff Williams took another sip of coffee.

I stood near the front entrance of the police station next to Murray, Detective Keene, and an anxious sheriff. A box of journals taken from Sarah Henson's closet was resting between us. They seemed like innocent leather-bound pages, but what was written on them could've sprung Bison Creek into an early apocalypse. Those journals were like mini bombs waiting to explode and leave our tiny mountain town in ruins.

"See you." Detective Keene stood with his arms crossed.

Murray followed his father's example and sipped coffee to pass the time.

"Okay," I sighed. "Look, we've got to talk about it sooner or later."

"I agree," Detective Keene responded, talking over me. "I'm not from around here so I think *I* should do it."

"You?" Sheriff Williams stood up straighter. "You have no business going through those." He gestured at the stack of journals. "What we should really do is burn them all."

"You'd be tampering with evidence if you did that," Detective Keene pointed out. "I'd be forced to report you to the proper authorities."

"I said it's what we *should* do." Sheriff Williams sneered at him. "Not what we're *going* to do."

"Keep those things under lock and key, Sheriff. I'm not kidding." I tapped my foot.

Over the space of about ten years, Sarah Henson had taken it upon herself to be the eyes and ears of Canyon Street, and who knew what sorts of secrets lurked within the pages of her diaries. After the sheriff had arrived at Sarah's house along with Detective Keene, he had insisted that we search the house thoroughly. Cydney had found something even more spine-tingling in Sarah Henson's attic—a vast collection of binoculars, maps, listening devices, and a clear view of Canyon Street.

She hadn't just been spying on some*one*, she'd been watching the entire town.

It would be time-consuming to skim through every single journal, though someone had to do it. But all of us were a little leery of spotting our own names. I could tell by the look on the sheriff's face. His cheeks were pale like he was being haunted by a poltergeist. And I was pretty sure that letting Detective Cydney Keene be privy to that sort of information was out of the question.

"I intend to." The sheriff stroked his gray mustache.

"So Sarah Henson was some sort of spy?" Murray said. "Do you think she was in league with Triads or something?"

Sheriff Williams shook his head.

"Why would the Chinese care what type of doughnut you eat every morning?" Detective Keene looked him up and down. "You should be wearing a clown suit."

"Enough," Sheriff Williams barked.

"Well, you three will have to figure this out on your own," I responded. "I need to swing by the groomers' and then head to work. Taryn, the other trainer, can only cover for me for so long."

"Hey, maybe we should give the books to Essie?" Murray nodded, the sweat on his forehead glistening. "You can keep a secret, right?"

"I'm a part-timer, remember? It would take me months to get through those."

"And she has no formal training," Detective Keene added. He glanced down at his own biceps as he crossed his arms.

I might not have had any formal police training, but at least I knew what to look for. I pretended that Cydney's comment didn't bother me, and turned my head toward the sheriff instead.

"I don't know what you'll find in there, but what you *don't* find is what matters." My mind flashed back to the mess in Sarah Henson's closet, and the one journal I'd found out of place. It had definitely had some pages torn out. "Figure out who's *not* in those books, and that'll tell you who the missing pages are about. Find that person, and you'll find who broke into Sarah Henson's house…and possibly her killer, too." I paused to let the three of them process the information. "Maybe the best thing to do here is divvy them up. You know, share the burden?"

"Unless you two have something to hide?" Detective Keene glared at Sheriff Williams and his dubious son.

"Is that what you think?" Sheriff Williams scowled. His boots made heavy thuds on the floor as he walked toward Sarah Henson's secret journals and began flipping through them. He handed one to Detective Keene, keeping a tight grip on the spine. Detective Keene yanked it out of his hands.

"I've seen it all, Sheriff. Nothing this bored old woman wrote will surprise me." Detective Keene cleared his throat and started skimming the first few entries. Sheriff Williams placed his hand on the page, blocking Cydney's view.

"You must promise me something, boy." The sheriff's voice boomed, and his bitter tone sent shivers down my spine. "You can *never* speak of the things you read in these books outside of the station. No one is to find out that this town has been hosting a spy for the past ten years. *No one.*"

"Yes, sir." Detective Keene gulped.

"How would you like it if these books contained records of *your* every move?" The sheriff took a step closer to Detective Keene, keeping his voice low and gruff. Detective Keene shifted from foot to foot, uncomfortably. "All I would have to do is open up a page to read what time you left for work this morning. Where you stopped for coffee. Who you talked to. What you wore on your evening jog last night."

Detective Keene didn't answer.

The thought of it made me queasy.

But I had nothing to hide.

"Big brother's watching," Murray joked with a snicker.

I didn't know who Sarah Henson really was, spy or civilian, but I did know that she must've found whatever she'd been looking for. And she'd paid the ultimate price—her life. All I could do now was listen and hope.

Listen for the howls of two lost Akitas.

And hope that my loved ones didn't have skeletons hanging in their closets.

* * *

Taryn flicked a strand of her hair, showing off her new look. One that I knew Mr. Kentworth would give me a hard time for. Taryn, the first trainer I'd hired when I was made lead fitness trainer at Pinecliffe Mountain Resort, sported light blue streaks in her hair. Taryn was an out-of-towner. Or, in other words, she couldn't have cared less about town politics. In fact, I admired the spirited way in which she spoke to people—like the mayor's wife, chairwoman of the Bison Creek rumor mill.

"My little sister dared me to do it," Taryn said, searching the storage closets for another medicine ball. "I know I look twelve."

"I kind of like it," I admitted. "It's different than what I see around here."

"Different means weird." Taryn raised her eyebrows.

The private fitness studio was on an upper level of the hotel, and it had two windows overlooking Canyon Street, the sparkling mountainside, and *of course* the parking lot. Business had been steady until about a month ago when the hotel was rocked by its first ever murder scandal. The result was a prime spot on the national news.

Now, the phone wouldn't stop ringing.

"Any updates on that new weight rack I ordered?"

"It should be delivered any day now," Taryn answered. "That is, if the roads don't ice over. Oh, and *he* wants to see you again in his office. He poked his head in here this morning."

I rolled my eyes. If Mr. Kentworth wasn't the owner of the resort and my sister's boss as well as mine, I'd ignore his request altogether.

"Warm up my first client if I'm not back in time," I responded.

"You got it, boss."

I took the stairs to the bottom floor of the hotel to get to Mr. Kentworth's office. A staff hallway ran along the back of the building, giving us all complete access to every part of the hotel without interrupting paying guests. There was a break room with employee lockers which I sometimes used, and a lounge area that some of the servers loitered in to play on their phones.

As I walked the hallway on the lower level, the scent of baked breads and sweet rolls filled the air. Brunch was being served in the dining room—the kitchen's regular assortment of lemon poppy seed bagels, blueberry scones, and cinnamon rolls. The smell tempted me to do some baking of my own, a dangerous game for someone who enjoys raw batter more than the finished product. I'd end up consuming way too many calories in one sitting.

"Oh, Essie." A young server with slicked back hair approached me. Eli was known for changing up his hairstyle pretty frequently. He was also known for pawning off his work on everyone else. It was a miracle Mr. Kentworth hadn't threatened to fire him because of it. I had a theory that the two of them were related, but I wasn't gutsy enough to ask. Both of them had long, lanky limbs, and swayed back and forth when they walked.

"Hi, Eli."

Eli thrust a box into my hands. I read the label—*Sugar Mountain Co.*

"Take this to Aggie in the kitchen, will you?" Eli grinned—a twisted sort of smile that made it hard for me to refuse.

"Eli, I don't have time—"

"Please, I'd owe you one." He sped past me without a backward glance.

"Fine," I shouted out him. "But if I find out you're dumping work on me so you and Misty can make out at spa reception, you're not going to like…" Eli had ventured too far to hear the rest of what I had to say to him.

The cardboard box was heavy in my hands as I headed toward the hotel kitchen. Aggie Korston was the head baker and all the kitchen staff made a conscious effort to stay on her good side. In fact, the only person who dared tiptoe on her nerves was Eli. And that was because he had the habit of sneaking through the kitchen at random times during the day and stealing a dinner roll. Or two.

"Aggie?" I entered the bustling kitchen, knocking on her closet of an office.

"Yes?" Aggie opened her door, still seated at her desk, and took a deep breath. Her chef's jacket was hanging on the wall, and her burly forearms—arms that could frost cakes for days—flexed as she typed at her computer. She fiddled with the rim of her reading glasses as she eyed the package in my hands.

"This was sent for you," I responded, failing to mention the name of the boy who had failed to deliver it. It might have set her off.

"Eli," Aggie murmured, shaking her head. At the mention of his name she pulled a circular tin from her drawer and rubbed a dab of violet-colored balm into her wrists. She closed her eyes, inhaling the soft scent on her skin.

"Lavender?" I guessed.

"It's lavender balm for stress relief," she replied. "The smell is supposed to calm the nerves. Flossie gave it to me yesterday. I think it's really starting to help me."

"I'm sorry. Flossie?" I hadn't heard the name before.

"Flossie Wicks, but you might remember her as Florence." Aggie's eyes widened as if I should've known who she was talking about. I shrugged. "She's an herbalist, and she's in town visiting her brother Booney, while stirring up trouble for the poor doc in the meantime."

"How do you mean?"

"Well, she claims she can give folks better results with herbs and such." Aggie sniffed her lavender balm again and shoved it back in her drawer. "Of course she also claims that she can speak to the dead, so...."

"It's been a long time since we've had a psychic living in town," I commented. The previous one, Madam Folliere, had mysteriously disappeared during the Bison Creek Wafflefest a few years ago after predicting that the world would come to an end on the previous day. She had later declared that she'd miscalculated the date.

"Whatever she is, her advice has been working for me so far." Aggie reached for the box. "Let's see what we've got here."

"I hear you're entering the Sugar Mountain Bake-Off," I said as she opened the package. The contents of the box included an entire range of Sugar Mountain baking equipment, everything from whisks to muffin tins.

"Mr. Kentworth says I can keep the prize money if I win. All he wants is the publicity." She studied each item like they were new musical instruments waiting to be tuned. "Personally, I just think he wants to piss off the Silverwood Hotel. Rub it in their faces that we were picked to host the event instead of them."

"Is it really that big a deal?"

"Don't know and don't care," Aggie responded. "I've never understood our rivalry with Silverwood."

"Me neither."

I glanced at the time, hoping the *I have a client waiting* excuse was enough to keep Mr. Kentworth from scolding me for not showing up at his office. As I glanced at my phone, it started to buzz. A name flashed on my caller ID. It was the name that had seemed to bring out the best *and* the worst in me. My stomach leaped, and I dashed out of the kitchen as fast as I could.

He called.

"Patrick," I answered the phone, trying to sound casual. My chest drummed regardless.

"Essie." Patrick's voice filled my head with a mix of emotions. His deep hazel eyes were burned into my memory. They were eyes that took me back to my childhood—the good times and the messy. "How are you?"

"Fine." I was grinning so wide that my cheeks started to hurt. "How's the shoulder?"

"In a sling for now," he answered. "I'll be off my snowboard for a while."

"Ouch." Boarding was Patrick's life, and his career. I imagined that starting the day without his morning run on the slopes was like my going a day without a good workout. "Sorry."

"I'll live." He gave a little laugh. "So listen, is it too soon to ask you to meet me tonight?"

Too soon? It's not soon enough.

"No," I blurted out, a little too quickly.

"Good, because I've got a few things I want to tell you."

"The Grizzly?" I suggested, knowing that inviting him over to my apartment would probably be a night spent cleaning poo from the floors or keeping Miso from chewing up Patrick's shoes. Miso was back at the apartment for the time being, and hopefully being looked after by Wade.

"Sounds perfect."

CHAPTER FIVE

I was confident that things between Patrick and me
would work out right this time. I left my apartment with
my chin held high and walked down the street toward
the town's local pub, the Grizzly. It was a place that the
locals called home. A place to wind down after a hard
day of tourist-pleasing. The bar held the same look it
had back when it was first built as the town saloon. A
long, wooden bar sat in front of a large framed mirror
that made the room look bigger than it actually was.
Antique liquor bottles decorated the walls, giving the
place an overall Wild West feel.

My eyes darted to every corner of the room as I
entered the bar. It was packed as usual, and loud
enough to hide the sound of my pounding chest. Patrick
hadn't arrived yet, giving me time to find a quieter
corner where the two of us could talk. I brushed elbows
with Doc Henry as I waved at the barman for my usual,
sparkling water with lime.

"Excuse me," Doc apologized. "Oh, Essie. What
brings you here?"

"I'm meeting a friend." It was a rarity to see the
doctor at the Grizzly after dark. He was the sort of man
who went to bed early after a light supper, the town's
model of healthy living. The doctor's drink sloshed in
his hand as he temporarily lost his balance. "Are you
okay?"

"Take a picture, Essie." Booney, columnist at
the *BC Gazette*, swooped in and patted Doc Henry on

the back. "You won't see the doc in here until the next full moon." Booney let out a shrill cackle and continued on his way to the bathroom.

"Rough day?"

"Rough week," the doctor responded. "And the week isn't even over yet."

"Yes." I nodded, wondering how fast word had spread of Sarah Henson's untimely death. "I know what you mean."

"I mean she has the nerve to come in here, and tell *me* how to run my practice?" He gulped down more of his drink, cringing from the bitter taste between his lips.

"Okay, I guess I don't know what you mean," I admitted.

"I should tell her to shove it up her chakras." Doc Henry attempted to laugh, but it came out as more of a raspy cough. "That'll teach her."

"Teach who?" I asked, observing the way his gaze wandered lazily from side to side.

"Flossie, that haughty cow. She's corrupting my patients." His expression changed like a flash of lightning. His eyes narrowed and he gritted his teeth as if Flossie herself was standing in the doorway taunting him.

"I'm sure it's not that bad." I placed a hand on his shoulder, trying to calm him down.

Don't suggest lavender oil.

"You know she told me to start dating again?" He held up his drink. "She said that my wife wants me to move on with my life. How dare she speak to me about Clara, may she rest in peace?" He took a step forward and almost knocked me over. The doctor didn't handle his liquor well.

"I'm sure she was only trying to be helpful," I replied.

Doc Henry flared his nostrils. He set down his drink on the nearest table and zipped up his coat. The door to the bar opened, letting in a cool breeze. The chatter throughout the room stopped, and suddenly every eye was on an overdue visitor.

"Well, by golly," Booney shouted from the back. "Look who's back from the dead."

Before Patrick could say anything, the bar erupted in applause. Patrick's cheeks turned scarlet as he nodded, stepping cautiously to avoid bumping his slinged elbow. It wasn't too long ago that Patrick was discharged from the hospital for a gunshot wound to the shoulder. It was also a lethal end to his engagement to a famous model. But no matter what lurked in the past, the residents of Bison Creek were proud of their local celebrity and pro-snowboarder, Patrick Jaye. *Former* pro-snowboarder, now that Patrick had decided to retire.

"Booney," Patrick muttered. Booney jogged toward him, leaving a whiff of spearmint and aftershave as he passed me. But his attempts to hide the smell of tobacco and booze never fooled anyone. Running the *BC Gazette* practically on his own, Booney was usually overstressed and overworked. "You haven't changed at all."

"Ladies and gentlemen!" Booney announced at the top of his lungs. He rested his hand on Patrick's good shoulder. "The man responsible for our current rise in profits. Our very own hometown celebrity, Mr. Patrick Jaye."

The room rang with more applause.

"Thank you." Patrick waved modestly, spotting me as he glanced around the room.

"It's been a long time since you've been in town for this long, son. Would you like me to tell you the story of how I lost my pinky in the war?" Booney held up his hand, where a small chunk of his pinky finger was missing.

"Which story?" Patrick answered. Booney let out a loud laugh along with half of the bar. It was a well-known fact that Booney liked to intimidate tourists who ventured into the local pub with a game of questions. Some made excuses and left, but some endured for most of the night and that's when Booney would break out his pinky story.

Except that the story changed every time he told it.

"I see you haven't forgotten us." Booney tilted his head, looking pleased. "Let me buy you a drink."

"Actually"—Patrick's eyes locked with mine— "I'm here to meet Essie."

"Oh," Booney responded, raising his eyebrows when he looked at me. "Of course."

I quickly tucked a strand of hair behind my ear as Patrick walked toward me. His blond locks were tousled and his eyes looked a brilliant shade of hazel. Tonight they were teetering toward a forest green with a hazelnut brown surrounding his pupils.

I found the nearest table and sat down. This was our first official date. Ever. We'd gotten together a few times with friends when we were teenagers, but Patrick had rotated through the girls on the track team back then. And I was just the quiet neighbor girl who used to help him build snow forts in the backyard.

"Hi." Patrick spoke first, pulling off the sleeve of his coat with one hand. The other side was draped snugly over his sling.

"Hi," I replied, my heart pounding like I was running on a treadmill.

"So, how's your no-caffeine thing going?" Patrick had remembered that I'd made a New Year's resolution to steer clear of coffee. January had been the hardest. But the withdrawal headaches and the mood swings got better. I'd made a lot of green and ginger smoothies.

"Still haven't caved," I answered. "How's the shoulder?"

"Painful at times, but it's healing." He rested his hand on the table and cleared his throat. "Essie, there's something I need to tell you."

"You can't possibly be keeping any more secrets," I joked. The previous month had been a whirlwind of a time for both of us. Not only with Patrick's broken engagement, but his mom was also undergoing cancer treatments. It broke my heart to see how thin and fragile she had become, but she was still the same Mrs. Anne from down the street who had taken the time to make her famous Mississippi Mud Bites the last time I'd seen her.

"Well, it's not really a secret." He chuckled, locking his eyes with mine. A look that took me on a stroll down memory lane. When Patrick and his family had moved in down the street they were the only southerners I'd actually met in person at the time. Now, I was used to his parents' accents.

"What is it then?"

"I'm going away for a while," he answered. "Mom's request. She wants to spend some time visiting family in Alabama before…" He bit the corner of his lip. "Before she starts her next round of treatments."

"Oh," I blurted out. I clenched my fists under the table. "When are you leaving?"

"Tomorrow." He sighed.

"Wow, so soon?"

"Time is precious these days," he said quietly. "At least, that's what my mom always says." He paused, studying my expression.

Our new beginning together wasn't off to a good start. In high school, I'd never had the guts to tell him how I really felt. Then he went pro in snowboarding, and I went off to college. I didn't see him for years until recently. When Patrick had finally realized there was a spark between us, it had been too late. He had already become engaged to someone else, and he'd chosen to honor his promise and move forward with a wedding.

Now I was single, he was single, and I couldn't stop thinking about that night on Canyon Street a few weeks ago when he'd kissed me. Everything around us had become a far-off blur in that moment. I remembered never wanting that kiss to end.

Why was our timing always off?

"Then, go to Alabama," I urged him, forcing a smile. "Don't worry about me. I'll just be here doing the usual."

"I wish I could stay," he replied. His eyes darted to his empty palm, and I quickly placed my hand next to his on the table. My heart raced as he reached for it—our fingers intertwining perfectly.

"I know."

He grinned, slightly squeezing my hand.

"Any chance you'll let me make it up to you?"

"That depends," I answered. "You said the same thing to me in second grade, and I ended up with a mound of dirt on my porch."

"You said you wanted an ant farm, but your mom said no."

"Yeah, and then I had a whole lot of sweeping to do," I responded.

"I promise not to leave dirt, or trash, or yellow snow on your doorstep." He squeezed my hand again, sending my heart rate soaring.

"Mrs. Tankle will be appreciative of that," I pointed out.

"I'm planning something for when I get back." Patrick leaned forward. The warmth from his hand shot up my arm and made my blood pump even faster. He made me nervous. We'd been neighbors and old friends for as long as I could remember, and he still had this way of making me stumble all over the place.

"Like a surprise?" I raised my eyebrows. "Will you give me a hint?"

"No way. I've already said too much." He tilted his head so that the light made his blond locks look like shimmering blocks of gold. "Actually, I probably shouldn't talk at all. I hear you work for the sheriff now."

"Sort of."

"Is this going to be a permanent thing?" he asked.

"I haven't decided yet." I sighed, wondering the same thing myself. "I really like my job at the fitness studio."

"But you are really good at investigating. Really." He took a deep breath. "I might not be here if it weren't for you." He adjusted his hurt shoulder and cringed. His "wedding day" hadn't been a pleasant one, but I'd been amazed so far at how well he'd seemed to process it all.

"It was a group effort," I added.

"Anyway." Patrick changed the subject. "I don't think you should rule it out."

"Can you imagine *me* in a uniform?"

Patrick winked, keeping a twisted grin on his face.

"Don't answer that," I said out loud.

"One of these days you'll have to let me in on your secret," Patrick responded.

My chest tightened.

What sort of secret?

"Who have you been talking to?" The question came out as a playful response, but the root of it was serious. I did my best to breathe normally, hoping that someone hadn't taken it upon themselves to air Sarah Henson's dirty laundry.

"Seriously," Patrick leaned in closer, "somehow you pick up on things I never notice."

Oh—that sort of secret.

My tendency to observe first and act later started in high school, or so my sister, Joy, had pointed out. I'd been a classic science geek—always asking why and dreaming up experiments in my head. Most of them involved the chemistry of baking. My edible research had been both my hobby and my high school boyfriend. It had also been a contributor to the spare doughnut around my waist. Instead of joining my hormonal peers on all of their crazy exploits, I stood by and watched. I'd convinced myself that it was better to learn from other people's mistakes, but really those had been my own insecurities talking.

And then college had happened.

"I've always been observant, I guess." I glanced across the bar. "In college, though, I was forced to kick it up a notch when my roommate thought her boyfriend was cheating on her."

"I see." Patrick nodded, looking impressed. "And?"

"He was," I added. "I suppose you could say that was my first official investigation—finding my roommate's boyfriend in a closet full of art supplies, with *his* roommate." I stuck out my tongue, having trouble swallowing that memory back down.

"Yikes." Patrick grinned.

"Yep. Just when you thought you'd heard it all, right?"

"So, what have you deduced about me?" he asked. Patrick's eyes softened as his gaze wandered over the curves of my face. I didn't have to deduce anything about him. I already knew him.

"All those magazines you've been in tell me everything I need to know," I joked.

"Okay, okay." He nodded, keeping a subtle grin on his face. He glimpsed over his shoulder at a woman sitting by herself at another table. "How about her? What can you tell me about her?"

"Seriously?" I cleared my throat, trying not to blush.

"Seriously," Patrick confirmed, raising his eyebrows.

"All right." I studied the woman, starting with her choice of attire. She was wearing a light-colored trench coat paired with a magenta scarf. Her nails were long, acrylic, and they matched the shade of her winter scarf. "Well, her nails have been professionally done, and they match her outfit." I eyed her shoes. "No ski coat or heavy-duty snow boots. If she's not a skier then I'm going to go out on a limb and say that she's in the beauty biz. A hairdresser probably?"

"Uncanny," Patrick commented.

"Of course, it helps when you've lived here long enough to know almost everyone by name." I waved a hand at the woman. "Hey there, Betsy."

"Ah, Essie," Betsy responded. "When are you coming in for a trim?"

"I'll call you."

Patrick shook his head, his eyes glinting in our dimly lit corner.

"Nicely played," he said.

The rest of our evening went by so quickly that Patrick hadn't even remembered to order himself a drink. The rest of the bar had disappeared around me, leaving just the two of us. We had too much to talk about, and too little time. Like reconnecting with a best friend after a lifetime of living apart.

Our walk back to my apartment above the Painted Deer Bookshop was bittersweet. Patrick's hand didn't leave mine all evening, even though our palms were both clammy. Flakes of snow sprinkled the two of us, and the chill mountain air cooled my burning cheeks.

"Good night, Essie." Patrick leaned in close. I could feel the heat of his breath on my face. It was like minty steam.

"Night." I glanced down at my keys. "Have a safe trip tomorrow."

"Thanks," he replied. His eyes wandered to my lips.

Kissing him should've been easy. We'd kissed before. But for some reason, my torso was frozen. Breathing wasn't second nature anymore, and I found myself struggling to stay relaxed. Thinking back to the last time we'd been this close, I remembered never wanting to let go of that moment. I'd wished that it would last just a little bit longer.

Patrick granted my wish, caressing the side of my cheek as he pressed his lips against mine. His touch lit a blaze that spread through my veins like wildfire. I instantly wrapped my arms around his sturdy neck and let him pull me closer.

Inside my apartment, something scratched the door.

A loud bark startled me, and I pulled away.
Miso.

"Sorry," I apologized. "Joy brought home a dog."

"Of course she did." Patrick laughed.

Miso barked again.

"I should…" I shrugged.

"Yeah," he agreed. "Don't want him waking up the entire block."

"Bye, Patrick."

I opened the door to my apartment and found Miso waiting, tail wagging. A note was on the kitchen table along with a half-eaten bag of Oreos. Joy was working late again, and the cookies probably equated to Wade's version of *I'll make us some dinner*.

"Looks like it's just you and me, Miso. Again." I slumped onto the couch, glancing back at the open bag of sweets. "You think there's any chance that Patrick will find some gorgeous southern debutante while he's away?"

Miso let out a soft bark as he jumped up and made himself cozy in the spot next to me.

"You're right," I replied. "I shouldn't be thinking about stuff like that. It stresses me out."

I took a second look at the open bag of Oreos.

"Joy," I muttered. "Why can't you hide your junk food the same way you do your liquor?" I slowly stood up. *Maybe just one?*

Miso followed me to the kitchen. I looked down at the colorful packaging—a chocolate crunch that was calling my name. Most people were able to stop after one or two cookies. Not me. In fact, one or two always turned into five or six. And five or six would turn into the rest of the bag because if you've already ruined your diet for the day, why not go all out? *Don't give in, Essie. Just walk away.*

This was why I used to seal the cookie dough ice cream with duct tape. I had my moments. Moments of madness and nervous binging. But I'd overcome them before. I quickly shoved the cookies into a cupboard as Miso whined. Instead, I pulled some frozen banana slices from the fridge. A treat I hadn't made in a while, but tonight definitely called for it.

Banana ice cream.

When my sweet tooth was out of control I made a chocolate version that tasted just as good as a scoop of creamy chocolate custard. I set up my blender, got out some cocoa powder, and the ingredients I needed to make my sugarless, no-bake brownie balls. The perfect topping.

Patrick will be back before I know it, right?

CHAPTER SIX

I wiped the drool from the corner of my mouth and groaned as I forced myself up off the couch to the sight of Joy munching on the last of her crunchy chocolate cookies. She narrowed her eyes as she studied me, shoving another Oreo into her mouth while ignoring Miso's pleas for a tiny taste.

"Up late or out late?" Joy questioned me. She was wearing her usual work attire—a pencil skirt and a long-sleeved blouse that covered the tattoos on her arms. Her dark hair was pulled back in a tight bun.

"Up late," I answered, taking a deep breath and stretching the kinks out of my neck.

"All right." Joy sighed, taking one last bite of her school-kid breakfast before tossing the empty package in the trash. "What happened?"

"What do you mean what happened?" I avoided all eye contact. Her glare was laser sharp sometimes. Almost painful. "We went out for a drink, and then I came home."

"And binged on health food?" she guessed. "But I see you passed the cookie test."

I rolled my eyes.

"Yes," I replied. "I do have *some* self-control." *Some.*

"You know one cookie won't hurt you, right?" Joy glanced down at Miso and scratched behind his ears. "I just want to make sure you understand that a teensy bit of junk food won't make you explode."

"I know," I admitted. "But—"

"But you can't eat just one," Joy finished. "I know. I know." She took a deep breath and raised her eyebrows.

"What?" I made a second attempt at stretching the muscles in my back as well as the stiffness in my neck. "Say it out loud."

"Oh, nothing." Joy hopped to her feet. It was rare that she kept her opinions to herself, unless she was speaking to her boss, Mr. Kentworth.

"Say it." I joined her in the kitchen, and Miso trotted to greet me with a swift lick of my fuzzy snowflake socks.

"I'm not a life coach or anything," Joy replied. "So, it's really none of my business."

"Spit it out or get over it," I answered, mimicking the exact phrase she'd uttered to me multiple times while we were growing up. Her harsh approach to dealing with feelings was one of the reasons she usually made enemies first and friends later. Luckily, she had me during high school. Part sister, part buffer for the many *false* accusations that had circled through our school's rumor mill—one being that she'd pierced her own nipple in the girls' bathroom, but had to take it out because it had gotten infected. I'd shut that rumor down pretty fast.

"Fine." She strutted to the pantry and pulled out a fresh bag of Oreos. Joy tore open the bag and grabbed a couple before sitting back down at the kitchen table. Miso's tail wagged as he kept his attention on Joy, and only Joy. "I've never seen you conk out on the couch before."

"So?"

"*So*, what happened?" Joy asked. "Did Patrick say he needs some space?"

"Not exactly," I answered, grabbing a glass of water. "He's going away for a while to visit family." I paused, processing her scrutiny. Patrick was leaving at his mother's request to see family. He wasn't taking off because he needed some space, was he?

"Okay." Joy wiped the crumbs from her blouse. She was still worried about my budding relationship with the town's golden boy.

"By the way, Miso could use a few things from the store."

"I know." Joy sighed. "So far I'm sucking at this whole dog-owner thing. I'm lucky I was able to swing by the corner market and pick up some dog food."

"Uh, *I* did that," a voice called from Joy's bedroom. Wade emerged with a toothbrush in hand. And not much else.

Miso growled.

"Honey," Joy said through her teeth. "What part of *clothes at all times* didn't you understand?"

I was impressed with how calmly the words left her mouth, but her cheeks turned rosy. I turned my back to the living room, and the oblivious look on Wade's face as he posed in his birthday suit. Nudity never did seem to bother him, and the sight of him standing casually like he was ready to leave for work was nothing new. I'd seen Wade at his barest many times before. Each time was less and less of a shock to the system.

"Oh." Wade chuckled as I covered my eyes. "Sorry, sweetpie, I guess I forgot."

"You *forgot* you were naked?" Joy raised her voice slightly—the precursor to one of their shouting matches.

"Well, yeah." Wade shrugged.

"Really?" Joy bit the corner of her lip to keep herself from yelling. "The roads outside are iced over. There's a draft coming through the gap in the front door. We have a new pup who might mistake your *you-know-what* for a chew toy, and you just forgot you weren't wearing any clothes?"

I pressed my lips together to keep from laughing.

Are they really going to fight about this right now?

"That's what I said." Wade stretched his arms over his head.

"Ugh, you—"

"Okay, *darling*, I will put some clothes on." Wade didn't shout back at all. As usual, he kept a sly smirk on his face. "And you two ladies are late for work."

While heading toward my room, I did my best not to look in Wade's direction. But he walked toward the kitchen anyway. I wrinkled my nose as he brushed past me to reach the fridge.

"Wade," I blurted out. "I mean this in the nicest way possible...please, move out."

CHAPTER SEVEN

My session with my last client of the day ended just in time. I tugged at the edges of my coat as I walked down Canyon Street toward a shop I didn't visit very often. The Bison Creek Bakery had a line coming out of the front door, even though the shop was closing soon.

I'd decided, after a long afternoon of squats and lunges, that I needed a distraction while Patrick was gone. Every time I closed my eyes, glanced out the window, or had a minute to think, all I saw was his face. His voice echoed in my head, repeating our last conversation. He never did tell me what sort of surprise he had in store for me when he got back. He never even hinted at what it could be. I got so caught up thinking about him that I had accidentally knocked over the basket of coffee creamers in the staff lounge.

I needed a distraction.

I needed to throw myself into police work.

The smell of fresh pastries wafted through the air as I pushed past a cluster of customers to get to the front counter. I grinned, noticing that Ada's latest sign that she'd posted in the window had already been taken down—*Honk if you're feeling peak-y*. Ada Adley was in no way like her mother, the head baker at the shop. Ada wasn't sweet. She didn't smile and say good morning to her regulars. She was...well, she was Ada. A starving artist stuck working the front counter at her family's bakeshop because she blew all of her money living in the big city. At least, those were the rumors.

My phone buzzed in my pocket as I approached the front counter that was filled with pastries—a variety of doughnuts, scones, sweet breads, and cupcakes. Sometimes there were giant sugar cookies bigger than my hand displayed by the register, but not today. *Good. Less temptation.*

"Hello?" I turned to face the frosty storefront window as I answered.

"Essie," Murray replied, "I hope you're coming in tonight."

"Of course," I responded. "I'm gathering more information right now, and then I'll stop by the station. How's the journal reading going?"

"Honestly?" He slightly lowered his voice. "Slow and...a little creepy. It appears that Sarah Henson had eyes *everywhere*."

"Weird." I glanced upward, observing the bakery ceiling for a hidden camera of some sort. "I'll be there soon, Murray. I promise."

"Until death do us part?" he joked. Sometimes he still referred to the Valentine's Day card he gave me in the fourth grade that said *Will you marry me?* It was cute back then, but not so much now. Especially since Murray still lived with his parents, and I was pretty sure his mother even packed his lunches for him most days. Who cuts their own sandwiches into miniature triangles?

"Don't push your luck." I hung up and watched Ada pour coffee for the next customer in line. Her stringy blonde hair was tied back, not braided like it normally was. Her skin was pale, which made the vibrant orange on her lips pop against her complexion.

She raised her eyebrows as I approached her—this was her version of a friendly smile.

"Essie." Ada sighed. "Let me guess, low-fat bran muffin?"

"Information."

"Ah, yes." Ada nodded at her next customer, carefully listening to his order of a dozen doughnuts and a slice of chocolate zucchini bread. "I heard you were the new hired help. Now you'll be paid to be nosy."

"If you call investigating a murder the same as being nosy."

"Sarah Henson?" Ada replied. She paused, giving me her full attention.

"When was the last time you saw her?" I asked. "Did she do her usual morning walk with the dogs on Monday?"

Ada stared at the register for a few seconds. Her bright orange lipstick looked like two slices of tangerine stuck to her mouth. She pressed her lips together, smoothing the splash of color more evenly around her pout.

"Come to think of it, no. I didn't see her on Monday." Ada took a deep breath. "I also could've missed her. I've been using every spare second I've got revising my recipe for the Sugar Mountain Bake-Off."

"*You're* entering the bake-off?"

"Don't look so surprised," she scoffed. "I do work in a bakery, you know. And unlike the rest of these butter-loving townies, I'll be entering something dairy-free. Mom thinks it can't be done without losing valuable points for taste."

Ada's next customer frowned as she studied the selection of pastries behind the glass.

"So you'll be serving *air* to the judges?"

"My special vegan oatmeal cookies," Ada answered. "The judges won't even know the difference."

"I guess everyone around is gunning for that cash prize."

"I heard that there are even a few entrants from Silverwood," she whispered.

"Absolute madness."

Ada rolled her eyes and retreated closer to the register.

"Sarcasm is a defense mechanism, Essie," Ada said casually. "It's in all the textbooks."

"Excuse me," a customer interrupted us, leaning over the counter. The woman who had been studying a cookies 'n' cream cupcake was now eyeing the color of Ada's lips. She clutched her leather handbag, a shiny black that matched her boots. "Where did you get that lipstick? I can never find colors that look as bright on my skin as they do in the tube."

"I made it," Ada responded. "Otherwise I would have to drive all the way to Denver to find a decent cosmetics store."

I wrinkled my nose. I guessed she was discounting the outlet mall in Silverwood.

"You're joking," the woman gasped.

"No, ma'am. All you need are crayons and coconut oil." Ada kept a bland expression as she recited the steps of her DIY lipstick project. "Melt an inch of crayon with half a teaspoon of coconut oil in a double boiler, and then pour it into a small container. It's simple."

So Ada really did paint, or color, her lips on this morning?

"I'll have to try that." The woman smiled and proceeded to order half a dozen cupcakes and a coffee to go.

"Is that all?" Ada asked. The woman standing at the register looked confused, but Ada glanced at me. "Essie, is that all?"

"For now." I smiled at Ada's current customer and tugged the collar of my jacket. So far my only leads were Sarah Henson's spy journals, and the safe that Sheriff Williams couldn't open. Maybe if we cracked the safe, we'd crack the case.

CHAPTER EIGHT

"What's the verdict?" I waited for someone to speak first. Sheriff Williams scratched the side of his chin. His pinky finger twitched and his eyes darted to the front window. It was time for his smoke break.

Detective Keene sat at his desk with perfect posture. Even his office etiquette was by the book. I glanced at the time, avoiding eye contact with Murray, who was slowly shaking his head.

"I can't believe you didn't bring me anything," Murray muttered, staring down at the closed journals on his desk. "You were at the bakery, and you didn't bring me anything."

"Buying you the last chokecherry scone didn't exactly cross my mind," I answered. "I was seeking out more information about what Sarah Henson was up to on the day she died."

"All you had to do was keep the receipt, and Pops would've reimbursed you." Murray shook his head, leaning back in his seat and grabbing another one of Sarah Henson's journals.

Detective Keene briefly looked up, long enough to shoot Murray a scowl.

"How many more have you got?" I asked.

"The stack's over there." Cydney nodded to a pile near the sheriff.

"So far just about everyone in this town has been mentioned," Murray commented. His dad glared at him until a bead of sweat formed above Murray's eyebrow. He took a deep breath and continued working.

I gulped, wondering what sort of secrets had been unleashed in this very room. I had nothing to hide, but my chest went tight.

The sheriff pushed aside his homework and rubbed his eyes. "We're going to need more time," he said.

"And in the meantime the killer is parading around town right under our noses," Cydney chimed in.

"What about the safe?" I asked. "Maybe that'll tell us more."

"The safecracker is booked until the weekend," Sheriff Williams answered.

"How about we take that hunk of metal out back and force that thing to open?" Murray suggested.

Cydney narrowed his eyes and glared at him.

"Because that would be in violation of—"

"Eh!" The sheriff jumped to his feet for dramatic effect. "No arguing. No bickering. No complaining. No nothin', understand, boys?"

"I understand, Pop." Murray nodded.

Detective Keene rolled his eyes.

"And you're positive *everyone* in town has been mentioned at least once?" I reiterated.

"Pretty close," Murray replied. "Although I haven't read anything about you, Essie."

"Maybe *she's* the murderer?" Cydney raised his eyebrows.

"That would be absurd." Murray straightened the collar of his uniform. "Essie is one of us now."

"The mayor," Sheriff Williams blurted out. The three of us looked at him, waiting for an explanation. "The mayor is not in these journals as of yet."

Detective Cydney Keene clenched his jaw, glancing down at his boots. According to the sheriff, he was related to the Millbrecks—a surefire embarrassment to his badge if one of his own relatives was guilty of murder. My mind raced back to my recent encounter with Mayor Millbreck at Patrick's wedding dinner. He'd spent most of the night chatting with Patrick's fiancée about red carpets and spray tans. It had been his wife, Martha, who had given me the most trouble that night. She'd threatened me to keep quiet about her love-capades with another man.

Though the air was chilly outside and a draft seeped in from under the door, my cheeks went hot. I pressed my lips together and watched the others process the sheriff's suspicions. If Mayor Millbreck was pegged as a murder suspect, the entire town would be in an uproar, including the many VIP guests he dined with every evening at the Pinecliffe Mountain Resort.

"What about Martha?" I inquired. My stomach churned as the sheriff shook his head.

"No, nothing about Martha either."

Sarah Henson was a crappy spy if she didn't know about Martha's affair. The two of them were even friends. But then again, maybe Martha's affair was on the missing journal pages. Maybe the Millbrecks weren't just a showy, scandalous, political couple. Maybe they were killers, too.

"Really," I said, clasping my hands together.

Cydney directed his scowl at me next.

"So that's it, huh?" The detective raised his eyebrows, quickly glancing toward the sheriff. "The mayor and his wife are missing from these journals, therefore *they* are our main suspects? Nice detective work."

A dull pulsing in my temples grew stronger and stronger. I rubbed the side of my head, trying to prevent a full-blown migraine from taking over my thoughts. But it was impossible with Cydney in the room. *I should start carrying a pill box.*

"If you think about it logically, it does seem suspicious." I took a deep breath, and forced myself to keep calm.

"Okay, then *logically* so do you, Essie."

I ground my teeth.

"Talk to my sister and her ex-husband," I replied. "They'll confirm where I was at the time of the murder."

"You wouldn't be the first killer to devise a clever alibi." Cydney smirked, sending my growing headache into overdrive. What had started out as irritating little pinpricks now felt like a constant pounding in my skull.

"Of course you're quick to defend your family," I retaliated. "After all, they are the reason you even have a job here in the first place."

Detective Keene jumped to his feet, and my heart leapt, too. I had struck a nerve, and he couldn't deny it. The ruby red color of his cheeks was proof of it.

"If you two don't cool it, I'll fire a warning shot." Sheriff Williams was on his feet, too. His weathered hands were close to his belt. It seemed that

Sarah Henson was causing more trouble in death than she had when she was alive. She'd been the quiet sort of woman who had kept most of the details of her life to herself, with the exception of the daily happenings of her two dogs. Now that there was no keeper of her journals, the contents could start wars between the friendliest of families in this town. In this case, the pen was definitely mightier than the sword...or whatever it was that the murderer had used to kill her.

"Sorry, Sheriff," Cydney said through his teeth.

"Now, if we find a lead we are going to follow it," the sheriff clarified. "I don't care who the suspect is. Let's cross more names off our list, shall we?"

"Yes, Sheriff," Cydney agreed. And probably only because it was protocol.

"Essie?" Sheriff Williams glared at me next. The way his skin drooped around his eyelids made his dark brown irises look midnight black. He looked like an angry grizzly.

"Yes, Sheriff," I answered him. "I have a training session with Martha on Friday. I can ask her a few questions then."

"And now we're getting somewhere." Sheriff Williams hovered near Cydney's desk long enough for the detective to take a seat. "In the meantime, it's back to the books while we wait for the safecracker."

Murray chuckled, flipping through the pages of one of Sarah Henson's journals like it was a gossip magazine. He scratched the side of his chin the same way his father did, and he kept a grin on his face as if it were another ordinary Wednesday.

"I can't believe that Stella Binsby over at the corner market does all her shopping in Silverwood,"

Murray commented. "It makes you wonder why her produce is always on sale." He chuckled again. "Oh, and Mrs. Tankle drives to Crystal City once a month to play the slots. No surprise there."

"Son, keep the commentary to yourself." The sheriff tapped his fingers on his desk and eyed his top drawer.

"Oh, here's one about you, Pop." Murray kept reading like the tension in the room didn't exist. The longer he giggled to himself like an immature schoolboy, the more the mood in the office lightened up. "Did you really meet with Flossie last week up on Pinecliffe Trail?"

"There's a woman in this town who calls herself Flossie?" Cydney muttered to himself.

"That is none of your concern," the sheriff answered.

"Is this one of those things I shouldn't tell Mom about?" Murray responded. "Like how you hate her cabbage casserole?"

"Hot dogs and cabbage shouldn't even be on the same plate," he retorted.

I covered my mouth to stop a burst of laughter.

"But you'll eat macaroni and ketchup," Murray added, shaking his head.

"I'm not having this discussion right now," Sheriff Williams said sternly. "Yes, I met with Flossie, okay? I admit it."

"What for?" Murray wasn't as hesitant to push the sheriff's buttons.

"That's *my* business." The sheriff stuck out his jaw and held his head proudly.

I came home to the sight of Miso wagging his tail. My apartment was quiet, but that didn't always mean it was empty. I shut the door behind me to keep the cold from sneaking inside. I scratched Miso behind the ear and unzipped my coat.

"Hello?" I called out. "Joy? Wade? Is anybody here?" I waited for a reply, but the apartment remained silent. "Or more importantly, is everybody clothed?"

I moved toward the kitchen and spotted a bowl of dog food and water on floor. Miso's leash was draped across the head of the couch, and a note was on the kitchen table. It was Joy's handwriting—an explanation as to why she would once again be home late. I glanced down at Miso, eyeing his shiny coat.

"You must be itching to get out of here," I said out loud. Miso wagged his tail as if he understood me. "Well, my shoes are still on…" Miso's eyes beamed as he stared at me. "All right, come on."

I grabbed Miso's leash and prepared myself to brave the cold again. I opened the front door, letting in a few flurries as I led Miso down Canyon Street. My shoulders tensed as we walked in the direction of Lake Loxley. The last time I'd ventured this way, Miso had sniffed out a deadly surprise.

This time Miso trotted at a slower pace. He didn't attempt to pull me forward like last time. He stayed close to my feet and studied every storefront we passed. I took a deep breath of mountain air, trying to think about anything but the one thing on my mind.

The one *guy* on my mind.

It seemed like only yesterday that the two of us were building snow forts in my parents' backyard. Patrick used to stay out in the snow until his mom begged him to come indoors. My fingers were like chubby little ice cubes after we'd played together, but Patrick always insisted that he was cold-blooded, a southern boy who was meant for the snow.

A sudden bark broke my concentration. Miso butted my calf with his nose, forcing me back onto the sidewalk. Mrs. Tankle's pickup truck slid on the road right next to me. My heart soared as she slowly gained control of her vehicle and resumed her evening drive down Canyon Street toward the neighboring street where she lived. I was in a daze again, but Miso had pulled me out of it just in time.

"You're a handy little guy, aren't you?"

I leaned down to pat the top of Miso's head, and he barked in reply.

CHAPTER NINE

My stomach churned as the clock ticked in the gym. It was Friday morning and Martha Millbreck would be arriving any time for her usual training session. I didn't want to be the one to have to ask her what her former gal pal had been up to, but someone had to do it. I just hoped Martha wouldn't resort to threatening me again. She was eager to chat about anybody's business but hers.

The door to the fitness studio swung open and Taryn escorted Martha into the room with a courteous smile. She often referred to Martha as *Blabby* Millbreck, and more than once I had to stop myself from blurting out her secret nickname.

"Good morning, Martha," I said. "Let's get started with a warm-up." It was my usual opening line, and so far Martha appeared to be her usual self. Her light brown hair was neatly pulled back, and her lips looked slightly swollen. *She's moved on from the Botox.*

"Morning, Essie," Martha replied, careful not to open her lips too wide. "I want to hear all about your hot date."

Taryn wrinkled her nose as she left the studio.

"What do you mean?" I gazed out the window at the snow-capped mountains.

"I heard you strolled into the Grizzly the other night and met with a certain someone." She raised her eyebrows as she hopped on a treadmill. Martha pumped her arms as she began walking, doing the best she could to get her heart rate moving without breaking a sweat. She avoided balling her hands into fists, and instead glanced down at them periodically. A shiny layer of strawberry red coated her nails.

"Who did you hear that from?" I asked, knowing that she could've heard it from anyone.

"Does it matter?" Martha grinned, checking her polish yet again.

"Not really." I shrugged. I had more important things on my mind, like why out of everyone in town, she and her husband were missing from Sarah Henson's spy journals. I eyed the speed on Martha's treadmill and turned it up a level. "A shame about Sarah Henson."

Martha took a deep breath.

"Yes, absolutely horrible." The tone of her voice wasn't as snide.

"She was a good friend of yours, wasn't she?" I glanced down at the workout I'd written down in my notebook, eagerly awaiting her response.

"I knew her better than most," Martha admitted. "It's shocking, isn't it?"

"What is?"

"How quickly life passes you by," she answered. "One day Sarah was here, and now…she's just a memory."

"When was the last time you saw her?" I kept my notebook open, ready to jot down anything that might be of use to the investigation.

"Oh, I don't know." Martha sighed, focusing her attention on the scenery through the glass in front of her. "Maybe a few days before she died."

"And she seemed normal?" I continued.

"Well, yes. Sarah was her usual self. An outright cold woman, except when it came to her dogs." Martha gave a little laugh and glanced at my notebook. My hands were clasping it a little too tightly.

"How do you mean?"

"Oh, that's right." She cleared her throat. "I suppose I should watch what I say in front the sheriff's new informant."

"That's an interesting choice of words," I commented. "Really, I'm just helping out with the investigation until the sheriff hires more officers. I know a lot of the locals, and Sarah Henson was once a client of mine."

"Then you know what I'm talking about." Martha turned down the speed on her treadmill. "Sarah wasn't the most social, but she knew a heck of a lot about dogs. By the way, what's become of her beloved Carob and Cayenne? Has anyone found them a new home? I wouldn't be surprised if she left them the house and all of her savings."

"We're still looking for them," I said quietly. The thought of losing Miso this time of year made my stomach queasy. If Sarah Henson's dogs had in fact wandered off, there were a number of reasons why they might never be seen again. First, there was the cold. Then, there was the wildlife surrounding the town.

"That's too bad." Martha brushed the side of her ponytail to make sure it was still smooth. "I actually liked those furry critters. They were very well-behaved just like my little Yorkie, Peppermint. More well-behaved than most of the children that run around town now."

"So, you must have an idea then? A theory as to who might've wanted her dead?"

"No," she replied. "I mean, I can't think of anyone in this town who would want to do her harm. Bison Creek residents are a peaceful people. It must have been an outsider."

"I wouldn't be too sure about that."

"Blame Silverwood," Martha resolved. "That usually works for me."

If the mayor of Silverwood were to be taken away in handcuffs, Martha would be one happy woman. I shook my head and turned the speed on her treadmill back to its original state. Martha resumed briskly pumping her arms.

"Where was the mayor Monday night?" I went on.

Martha tilted her head as she studied my expression. She stuck her lips out even more, making them look like a duck's bill. She took a deep breath and brought the treadmill to a dead stop.

"I came here for a workout, not a murder interrogation." She folded her arms, her cheeks flaming red. "I see Sheriff Williams has set his sights on poor Herald. He can't accept that he screwed up his last investigation so now he's taking it out on my husband."

"No, that's not it at all," I reassured her.

"Call me when you're back to playing fitness trainer, Essie." Martha gently wiped her forehead and headed for the exit.

My heart raced as I thought back to my agreement with Sheriff Williams. For some reason he trusted me, and Detective Keene would most likely rattle off *I told you so's* if I went back to the station empty-handed. I was hired because I could do the job, and I knew what made the people in this town tick.

Martha Millbreck was no exception. She was a woman who thrived on speculation. Rumors and threats of rumors were what made her tick, and she was forgetting one very important detail. I knew her secret. Whether or not her affair had been written in Sarah Henson's books, *I* knew what she was up to when she wasn't nosing her way around town.

But did her husband know?

"Stop," I called out. "Come back here, Martha, and answer my question."

"Not a chance, honey."

I was going to have to be more direct with her. She was used to telling *other* people what to do, not the other way around.

"Stop or I'll tell my landlady, Mrs. Tankle, all about your rendezvous with the gentleman in the black BMW. I think we both know what'll happen once that cat is out of the bag."

Martha stopped suddenly and slowly turned around to face me.

Game face, Essie. Don't cower.

"You don't have it in you," Martha replied.

"You could always chance it and find out." I stood my ground.

Martha paused, taking a brief minute to stare me down, but it didn't help.

"Fine," she muttered. "You're a big girl now. If you want to play with fire, that's your choice."

"Let's talk about the mayor." I jumped back to my main mission—to find out what the mayor was hiding. "Where was he Monday evening?"

"I could tell you that the two of us were having a quiet night in," she responded.

"But would that be the truth?"

Martha looked away as she shook her head.

"I don't know where he was Monday night," she admitted. "I wasn't home."

"I see."

"You're walking on very thin ice, Essie." Martha lowered her voice. "I hope you do the smart thing here, and don't go jumping to any conclusions."

"I'd have to say the same to you, Martha."

"Herald isn't capable of murder," she blurted out. "It wasn't him."

Martha's gaze wandered past me and out the window. Her eyes went glossy, and she gently dabbed at her eyelashes. I'd never seen her this way. She stayed quiet, letting her thoughts get the best of her. A tear ran down her cheek, and she quickly wiped it away. There was something going on. Something she didn't want to tell me.

Martha sniffled, forcing herself to smile.

"If you know something," I began, "just say it. You can trust me, Martha."

"Are we done here?" She raised her eyebrows. "I have somewhere I need to be."

"Whatever it is, it could help us solve this case much quicker."

"I am through discussing this," Martha responded. "And I would advise you to mind your own business from now on." Her nostrils flared.

"But Sarah was your friend," I went on. "I'm only trying to—"

"No!" Martha pointed at me as if I were a puppy chewing on her favorite pair of heels. "That woman *pretended* to be my friend, but all the while she was slinking around behind my back!"

The way her emotions took control of her was like watching Joy on the phone with the cable company. One minute she was fine, and the next she acted as if her entire world were falling apart.

Now I'm getting somewhere.

"I don't understand," I lied, hoping that the truth would finally come out. "I thought—"

"I'm sure you think I'm the scum of the earth, dear girl," Martha interrupted. "Yes, I'm having an affair, but the mayor drove me to it."

"Are you saying that—"

"Yes, okay?!" she shouted back. "Sarah Henson and my husband were fooling around."

CHAPTER TEN

The door to the fitness studio swung open, and Eli rushed inside. He bent over, placing his hands on his knees in order to catch his breath. He must have taken the stairs; the elevator was a little slow sometimes. Taryn jogged in next with a stern look on her face.

"Eli," she scolded him, "how many times do I have to tell you? You can't just burst into the gym whenever you feel like it. This isn't the kitchen."

"It's Mr. Kentworth," Eli blurted out.

Taryn crossed her arms.

"He can pick up a phone, can't he?" Taryn rolled her eyes. I held up my hand in an attempt to calm her down too, as Martha's wide-eyed gaze moved from Eli to me.

"Everyone, just settle down," I said. "Eli, tell Mr. Kentworth that I'm with a client and that I'll go see him in his office after lunch."

"That's not going to work." Eli took a deep breath. "I think he might be dead."

I bit my bottom lip and clenched my fists so tight my nails dug into my palms. A surge of adrenaline pulsed through my veins, but I glared at Eli. He was known for being more of a prankster than a reputable employee.

"Eli, if you're joking around—"

"No, Essie, this isn't a joke." Eli stood up straight. His eyes were wide and his voice was soft, not much louder than a whisper. "One of the guests found him outside. I called the sheriff, but I don't know what else to do."

Without another word the four of us all looked at each other. I ran out the door first, hearing footsteps pounding behind me. I focused on the staircase. There was no time to wait for an elevator. Not if there was the slightest chance that Mr. Kentworth was still alive.

I sprinted toward the main floor, skipping steps when I could. When I reached the staff hallway, I jogged past the employee lounge and break room and stormed outside into the frigid morning air. The cold pierced my bare arms like icicles. I searched the grounds from the parking lot to the main entrance to the resort.

"Over here!" Eli bumped my shoulder and began running as best he could through the icy parking lot. He slid more than once, but was able to keep his balance as if he were standing on a snowboard.

Mr. Kentworth was lying next to a powdery evergreen. He was face down in the snow, and the sight of his tall, thin body lying so still made my blood run colder than the ice in Lake Loxley. I was hesitant to touch him, not sure if he was alive or dead. A siren rang out in the distance, pulling me from the shock of the situation. I knelt down beside my employer and shook his shoulders.

"Mr. Kentworth!" I said loudly. "Mr. Kentworth."

Eli, Taryn, and Martha Millbreck were all behind me, watching. I gulped, slowly rolling Mr. Kentworth over so I could see his face. The snow had absorbed into his navy suit coat, and his skin was pale.

I felt for a pulse.

"Well?" Martha couldn't wait any longer. "Is he dead?"

I breathed a sigh of relief when I felt a dull pulsing in his neck.

"Today is your lucky day, sir," I muttered.

"Oh, thank heavens," Martha replied.

A car door slammed, and Sheriff Williams approached the scene.

"Eli, please tell me that you called an ambulance too." I paused, waiting for Eli to confirm.

"What?" He shrugged. "I thought he was dead."

"Don't just stand there, boy," the sheriff interjected.

Eli took off, skipping from snow patch to snow patch until he was back inside.

"What happened?" Sheriff Williams asked.

"I don't know." I shook Mr. Kentworth again, but it didn't rouse him from his slumber. I studied the sides of his head, looking for a mark similar to Sarah Henson's. His bones appeared to be intact but that didn't mean he wasn't attacked. "Was this an accident or another attempt by our killer?"

"No blood," the sheriff pointed out.

"He could have fought the killer off." I pinched his cheeks, hoping he'd open an eye. "I guess we won't know until he wakes up." My eyes darted to the landscape surrounding the parking lot. Not a single snowflake looked out of place.

But what was Mr. Kentworth doing outside in the first place? He normally spent the majority of his morning either in his or Joy's office, or hassling Aggie in the kitchen. As I inhaled the mountain air, shivers trickled up and down my spine. The cold was catching up with me.

"Come on, Mrs. Millbreck," Taryn said, taking Martha by the arm. "Let's get you back inside."

"I'm not *that* old." Martha yanked her arm back to prove her point.

"Okay," Taryn whispered to herself. The two of them made their way back indoors, leaving the sheriff and me to wait with Mr. Kentworth. I did my best to try and wake him up, but it was no use.

"Are you sure he's alive?"

"It was faint, but I know I felt some sort of pulse," I answered.

"Any luck with Martha?" Sheriff Williams scanned the parking lot as he talked to me, waving his hands when he spotted Doc Henry with his medical bag. He must have heard the sheriff's siren blasting down Canyon Street.

"Oh yeah." I watched the doctor make the climb toward the resort's parking lot. "She told me plenty, and Cydney, I mean Detective Keene, isn't going to like it."

"Don't tell me the mayor really had a hand in this." The sheriff cleared his throat.

"Well, he had a motive," I responded. "He and Sarah Henson were lovers."

* * *

I usually spent my Friday nights alone with a good book or a season of reality TV. Tonight I wasn't alone. There was a guy at the other end of the couch, and he stared me down whenever I didn't share my snacks.

Sure, he was furry and he had four legs, but he was still better company than the pizza delivery guy who showed up when Joy called in her usual order—ham, pineapple, and black olives—a Friday night staple when we were kids.

"Are you sure you don't want to come with us?" Joy said for the hundredth time.

"No," I replied. "I'm over being a third wheel, and I'm waiting for an update on Mr. Kentworth."

"A healthy threesome never hurt anybody," Wade joked, zipping up his jacket.

"I'm going to pretend you didn't say that." I glanced back at the television.

Joy and Wade were taking advantage of Joy's night off by going out to dinner. A dinner date that would probably end up with a late-night drink at the Grizzly, and maybe even breakfast at Ada's in the morning. Joy had only invited me along because it was the sisterly thing to do.

"Are you sure you'll be okay all by yourself?" Joy adjusted the hem of her sweater dress that she'd paired with bright yellow tights.

"Of course," I laughed. "You two go and have a good time."

"Okay." Joy sighed.

"And keep all the rowdiness far away from the bookshop. You never know if Mrs. Tankle is down there sorting through inventory."

"Right." Wade nodded. It was no secret that my landlady thought he was the devil in disguise. "I'll steer clear of her storefront this time."

"You'll let me in on what's going on with Mr. Kentworth, right?" Joy took one last look at me before leaving.

"Yeah, like if he is showing up for work tomorrow," Wade added, "because we might be wanting a morning in."

Joy clenched her jaw and gave him an icy stare.

"I'll keep you updated," I responded.

The two of them shut the door behind them. Miso sat up and studied the room for a few minutes before drifting back down to his previous position. I kept my eyes on the television, because otherwise they would wander to the kitchen. I'd received a couple of texts from Patrick, just a casual *how are you?* and *what's the weather like today?* No phone calls. It made me wonder what he was really doing on the other side of the country, and who he might be seeing—all speculation that would have led my past self into the arms of a cream-filled doughnut.

"Should I call him?" I said out loud. Miso tilted his head. "You're right. I don't want to seem too clingy. Or does not calling him make me seem too distant?" Miso tilted his head in the opposite direction. "I'm overanalyzing this, aren't I?"

Miso let out a low bark.

I turned off the TV and moved my focus from the chocolate drawer in Joy's bedroom to something more engaging. Mrs. Tankle often passed her used-book bargain bin to me to sift through. I had a bookshelf in my room filled with everything from romance to sci-fi. Miso followed me into my bedroom and hopped up on my bed as I chose my Friday night read.

As soon as my head touched the pillow, I had a hard time keeping my eyes open. My eyelids were heavy, and as soon as I took a deep breath and began reading about someone else's problems, mine floated away. My head drooped to the side until I couldn't fight the inevitable. Miso wedged his back up against my side, acting as a furry comforter.

Sometime later my eyes opened to Miso jumping off the bed and landing on the floor with a loud thud. The sudden noise startled me, and I sat up. My room was dark, and the rest of the apartment was quiet. I rubbed the sides of my arms as I followed Miso to the front door. He stood on his hind legs, attempting to turn the door knob on his own.

Joy and Wade must be back.

"Give them their privacy," I whispered. "They'll come inside eventually." I crossed my arms and waited, glancing at the clock on the kitchen stove. It was after midnight. "Actually, I'd say they're home early tonight."

Miso scratched at the door. I rolled my eyes, grabbing my coat and throwing on a pair of snow boots. I guessed he couldn't hold it any longer. I braced myself before opening the front door, ready to find my sister and her ex-husband in a deep lip-lock.

A gust of flurries rushed inside. My front step was empty, and it was snowing again. The steps leading up to my front door glimmered under the moonlight, and Canyon Street was silent apart from the distant glow of the local bar. Miso dashed from the front door all the way down to the Painted Deer Bookshop.

"Miso," I said under my breath. I slammed the front door and followed him. "Miso, get back here." I shoved my hands in my pockets and trudged through the snow. Miso stopped and began sniffing. My heart raced as he turned toward me and headed back toward the apartment. "*Miso.*"

Miso's midnight coat was covered in snowflakes. He shook his fur clean and resumed his tracking. Normally, he was quick when it came to doing his business. Tonight he was taking his time. Or maybe he got a whiff of a bighorn sheep.

Miso stopped sniffing long enough to glance down the street at the Pinecliffe Mountain Resort while baring his teeth. He growled—a rumbling noise in the back of his throat that started off low and grew louder. His teeth were in full view as his eyes glared into the night.

Or maybe he's seen a bear...

I took a few steps toward him and squinted my eyes. Canyon Street remained still and peaceful, as soft snowflakes continued to form a powdery blanket on the road and sidewalks. The snow had a way of cleansing its surroundings. The delicate frost had the ability to cover even the ugliest of landscapes. Canyon Street looked absolutely angelic, but looks were deceiving.

I glanced down and noticed something I'd almost missed.

There were footprints in the snow, and in a couple of minutes those footprints would be gone. Snowflakes dropped into the boot-shaped imprints, and I couldn't make out the rest. Thanks to the healthy dusting allotted to our tiny town by Mother Nature, it was like those footprints had never existed.

CHAPTER ELEVEN

"I've had enough of this," I shouted, gripping the handle on my snow shovel.

I hadn't slept all night. Miso guarded my bedroom door. His mood had changed after he'd ventured into the snow. He hadn't slept either. I'd tossed and turned until I finally closed my eyes, but the jingling of Miso's collar had awakened me.

"Whoa there, sis." Joy held her hands up in surrender. "What's with the snow shovel?"

It was Saturday morning, and I was a wreck. My head pounded like I'd spent the night at the Grizzly, but really it was the sleep deprivation. I lowered my weapon, trying to take a calming breath.

"Sorry," I mumbled.

"I had no idea you were just as crazy as your sister," Wade responded, heading toward the kitchen. "I kinda like it."

"Stay out of my corn chips," Joy called after him. She was still wearing her sweater dress and brightly colored tights. "I'm serious, babe."

"You two look like you had fun last night," I commented.

"If you call listening to Wade relaying his Sasquatch theories to Booney all night *fun*." She shook her head.

"He's real!" Wade added from the kitchen. He was already searching the fridge for a cold beverage.

Joy ran her fingers through her dark locks and bent down to pet Miso.

"But it was still a good time," Joy responded. "I take it you haven't heard anything about Mr. Kentworth?"

"I haven't checked my phone." My eyes darted to the front window.

"What's the matter?" Joy raised her eyebrows. Her gaze wandered from my mismatched socks to my crooked T-shirt.

"I don't know." I rubbed my forehead, hoping it would stop the pounding. "Maybe I was just imagining it, but Miso started acting weird, and then I went outside, and there were these footprints—"

"Footprints?" Wade interrupted. "Are you saying we've got a peeper, because I'm not okay with that."

"Says the man who walks around naked half the time," Joy muttered.

"I don't know," I replied, "but I hardly slept."

"We're here now if you need to crash." Joy nodded, ignoring the crunching coming from the kitchen.

"I can't. I've got to head over to the station. I've got a second job, remember?"

"I'm surprised you haven't figured out by now who whacked poor Sarah Henson," Wade commented.

"*Corn chips*," Joy muttered, glaring at him. Wade brushed the salty crumbs on his jeans and quickly put her chips back in the cupboard.

"It's not that simple." I took a deep breath. Though I wished it was that simple. I would have had a pocket full of cash by now, and I wouldn't have to put up with Cydney until my services were needed again.

"You're telling me," Joy mentioned. "I've been having the hardest time finding a replacement judge for the Sugar Mountain Bake-Off."

"What?" I paused, waiting for her to elaborate.

"Yeah, Sarah Henson was going to be one of the judges." Joy retreated to the kitchen for a tall glass of water. Miso watched her, wagging his tail. "Mr. Kentworth told me. Didn't I mention that?"

"Uh, no." My heart pounded as if I had downed a liter of coffee—something I hadn't had since New Year's Eve. "You didn't mention that little detail."

"Oh, sorry."

Joy shrugged like it was no big deal, but she was mistaken. If Mayor Millbreck had a solid alibi as to where he was on Monday night, then this was helpful information. It was another lead. A motive for a crazed participant to whack her—or his—way to the top.

Did someone in Bison Creek want to win the bake-off badly enough to kill for it? It wasn't until last month that I'd witnessed how far a seemingly normal person could fall.

"Do you have a list of the entrants for the bake-off?" I asked.

"Of course, the deadline to enter recipes has already passed." Joy eyed the time like she was late for an appointment. "The bake-off is next Saturday. Come Thursday night I definitely won't be sleeping. I still have a ton of work to do. The show must go on whether or not Mr. Kentworth will be there."

Before she finished talking, I'd raced to my room to get dressed. If Sheriff Williams wasn't up by now, I planned to bang on his door until he answered. Joy followed me to my room along with Miso. His collar jingled as he trotted to my closet.

"Email me that list of entrants," I said to Joy.

"Sure." She watched me curiously as I grabbed a pair of jeans and a thick scarf. "You're leaving *now*?" She tapped her fingers on my dresser. They were acrylic, and it was rare that I ever saw Joy without them.

"Why not?" I responded. "I can't sleep, and there's work to be done."

"When will you be back?" Joy glanced at a chipped corner of her nail as she spoke. *She has an appointment today.*

"I'll take Miso with me," I said.

"Oh, I—"

"Nail appointment?" I guessed.

"Is it that obvious?" Joy studied her faded polish.

"You act a bit like Mom when you have somewhere to be," I explained. "And since Mr. Kentworth is in the hospital the only other thing that would have you checking the time every other minute would be a trip to Betsy's."

"I do not act like Mom," Joy insisted.

"That's something Mom would say,too," I teased her. "Now, get out of my room before I tell on you."

Joy chuckled as she shut the door.

* * *

Miso wagged his tail all the way to the police station that was just off Canyon Street. He shook the snow from his midnight coat as I knocked on the door. It was early in the morning, too early for most of the town to be up and about. I pulled out my cell phone to call the sheriff, but a sudden noise stopped me.

Cydney had opened the door with a smug look on his face. His hair was gelled and parted to the side as usual. His work shirt was neatly pressed, and he looked as if he had been up for hours—bright-eyed and ready to pounce. He narrowed his eyes, glancing down at my furry companion.

"You're up early," I said. I cleared my throat, swallowing my urge to point out that hanging out at the station alone made him look a little guilty, since I knew it might result in a door slamming in my face.

"Ditto." His response was brief and to the point. He crossed his arms instead of stepping aside to let me in.

"Aren't you going to let me inside?"

"I haven't decided yet," the detective replied. "Are you going to accuse my mother's cousin of murder?"

"I take it the sheriff told you about the mayor's affair," I muttered.

Cydney rolled his eyes before finally standing aside. I stepped into the warm police station with Miso at my heels. The front room was dark with the exception of the glowing light on Cydney's desk. A folder of paperwork was open next to a steaming mug of coffee. Cydney strolled back to his seat where he'd been cross-referencing a couple of Sarah Henson's journal entries. My eyes immediately darted to his knees and how he tended to step heavier with his left foot, favoring his right side.

Dad does that after he mows the lawn.

"Mayor Millbreck's personal life is none of our business," he answered, carefully sitting back down at his desk.

"It is when his lover turns up ice cold in Lake Loxley." I took Murray's desk across the room, assuming he wouldn't be in for hours, especially if he was into Saturday morning cartoons.

"Just because someone is unfaithful doesn't mean he's a killer." Cydney resumed reading through the open journal entry in front of him. I unhooked Miso's leash and he sat quietly at my feet.

"Well then, you'd be happy to know that I have another theory as to who murdered Sarah Henson," I added. Cydney stopped reading and studied my expression.

"Go on. What is it?"

"I'll tell you when the sheriff gets here," I responded. Cydney frowned, scratching the side of his coffee brown hair.

"That could be hours from now," he argued.

"Then you'll hear about it hours from now." I couldn't help but grin when the eager smirk on Cydney's face was wiped clean.

"You're impossible, you know that?" He shook his head, but his opinion of me didn't matter. I had more pressing things on my mind than playing nice with Detective Keene.

"I'm pretty sure that snubbing the town consultant is against the rules."

"So is letting a dog run wild around the station," he quietly remarked. I stared at him blankly. Miso was quieter than a jackrabbit. "Wait until this town gets a proper sheriff. We'll see who's laughing then."

"Excuse me?" I blurted out, leaning forward in Murray's chair. Miso jumped to his feet, keeping a close watch on Cydney. "Sheriff Williams might not be the best, but I doubt the residents of Bison Creek will risk appointing a newcomer to do the job."

Cydney flipped through a few pages and gently sipped his warm java. The twisted smirk was back on his face, and he avoided looking up at me as if eye contact would give away his game plan. The sheriff had gone out of his way to accommodate him in order to avoid further conflict, and all this time Cydney had been plotting a plan of attack. Whatever that plan was.

"I'm sure you're right," Cydney responded without any argument. I wrinkled my nose at his reaction. What *was* his angle?

"But if you think you can do better, then by all means...."

Cydney kept his mouth shut, though I'm sure he did think he could do better.

He might change his mind when old man Simpkins starts bothering him with noise complaints.

My stomach churned as I picked up a journal that was sitting on Murray's desk. I opened it to page one and studied Sarah's loopy, cursive handwriting. I kept an eye on the clock, leaning down to scratch Miso's ears every couple of minutes. I couldn't relax with Cydney in the room. I didn't trust him, and I couldn't figure out why he had dropped everything to come to a little mountain town like Bison Creek.

About thirty minutes had passed before the sheriff finally walked through the door. His eyes were still heavy, and the tip of his nose was ruby red from the cold. He cleared his throat, observing the two of us at our desks.

"I'm glad you're both here," the sheriff stated. He glanced at Cydney. "After yesterday's discovery, I think it wise that we fully investigate Mayor Millbreck before we go any further. I want a good solid alibi out of him."

"Understood, sir," Cydney answered.

"You will visit him first thing this morning," Sheriff Williams continued.

"Absolutely." Cydney wasted no time arranging the paperwork on his desk into one simple stack before he reached for his coat.

"Essie, you're going with him." The sheriff hardly looked at me when he said it, probably knowing that I would complain about the company.

"Sheriff, I—"

"It has been decided." He cut Cydney off before he had the chance to protest. "The two of you will partner up today."

"I would rather go with Murray, sir. He's more experienced." Cydney clenched his jaw.

"Murray won't be in until later," the sheriff answered. "You will go with Essie."

"Or I can go alone?" Cydney suggested. "Essie was just telling me that she has a *new* lead. One that doesn't involve the mayor at all."

"Is that so?" Sheriff Williams raised his eyebrows, noticing the dog at my feet. Miso watched the sheriff just as closely as he had watched Cydney.

"I was talking with my sister this morning and she told me that Sarah Henson was supposed to be a judge at the Sugar Mountain Bake-Off."

"So you think someone might've bumped her off for a chance at the prize?" Cydney guessed.

"It's possible, isn't it, Sheriff?" I did my best to cut Cydney from the conversation completely. It took all I had to keep calm when all he did was question everything I said and did.

"Get a list of everyone in town who entered into that competition," the sheriff advised.

"I'm already on it." I nodded.

"Good." Sheriff Williams rubbed the side of his mustache. His hands automatically reached into his shirt pocket, the place where he usually kept his cigarettes. This morning his pocket was empty. "It looks like you two have a lot to do today."

"But—" I tugged at a strand of my hair.

"No *buts*." The sheriff waved his hand. "You can start your inquiries about the bake-off at the bakery. It should be open by now."

I couldn't avoid it any longer. I was about to spend the day with a man who would write me a ticket in a heartbeat if I did so much as jay-walk in his presence. I zipped up my coat, trying to stop myself from grinding my teeth too loudly. Only Miso noticed. At least I had him to vent to afterwards.

CHAPTER TWELVE

The sun peeked out from the Rockies, warming the sidewalks enough that patches of concrete showed through. It was a busy Saturday morning. The resort had been booked the night before, which meant crowded slopes on Pinecliffe Mountain and a rush of shoppers to the various storefronts on Canyon Street.

I paused just outside of the Bison Creek Bakery, scanning the list of bake-off entrants on my phone. Luckily, it hadn't taken long for Joy to forward me the info I needed before she'd left for her nail appointment.

"Geez," I muttered, keeping a solid grip on Miso's leash. "Apparently everyone and their mother is a baker in this town."

"Money makes people do crazy things," Cydney commented. He looped his thumbs on his belt, sizing up every tourist who hurried from shop to shop, gazing at window displays. Bison Creek had been busier than ever since it had appeared on the national news, and it was only getting busier. Pretty soon the sheriff would need a whole team of officers constantly patrolling the streets.

Maybe that had been the plan all along...minus Sheriff Williams as the acting sheriff?

"Five thousand dollars," I corrected him.

"Exactly," he emphasized. "That's a whole lot of money to some people." He turned to observe the look on my face. "You don't honestly think that every single resident in this town is innocent, do you?"

I didn't answer, mainly because I didn't have to. I'd grown up in Bison Creek, and I knew it backwards and forwards. It was a town full of memories for me. I couldn't imagine anyone in it committing such a terrible crime.

But I guess Cydney could.

"There's a whole lot of people on this list," I said, ignoring his question. "Too many to visit all in one day. Especially the few who live in Silverwood. We'll just have to start with the nosiest of them all."

"I can think of no other way to spend my weekend." Cydney let out a brief, sarcastic laugh.

I headed down Canyon Street toward my little apartment. Mrs. Tankle might have been elderly, but she caught on to a lot more than people thought she did. She loved listening in on her customers at the Painted Deer Bookshop, and she once told me that her husband came around to tea every Wednesday for a chat. Her husband had passed away when I was just a kid.

Naturally, Mrs. Tankle always had heaps of news. Real *and* imaginary.

"Come on," I urged him, walking at my normal pace—a little bit quicker than the average person. Cydney walked briskly beside me. His slight limp wasn't as subtle when he moved faster.

We reached the bookshop just in time to see my landlady through the frosted storefront window. I tapped on the glass until she noticed the two of us standing outside next to her window display. It held a stack of books so high that it looked like it might topple over, but Mrs. Tankle had glued them together a couple of years ago. She'd wanted her window display to have that *awe factor*, as she'd described it.

"I'm afraid I'm not open yet, dearies," she said, answering the door. She sized Cydney up immediately, squinting her eyes as if she needed glasses to clearly see his face. Miso wagged his tail in her presence, but Mrs. Tankle paid no attention. She was more of a cat person. "Oh, you must be the new detective I've been hearing so much about. Please, come on in." She glanced down at Miso's leash. "But—"

"I'll keep an eye on him," I butted in.

"Keep him away from Bing. She'll scratch his eyes out if he goes near her kittens."

Cydney looked puzzled as he followed me inside. The Painted Deer Bookshop was the kind of place where time didn't matter. It was so tight and cozy, with a comfy reading nook and bookshelves that touched the ceilings, that anyone could wander in and get lost in a good novel. I usually had that problem when I stopped in to check the bargain bin. I always lost track of the time when I was sorting through the new reads that Mrs. Tankle had put on sale. This time of year, her bargain bin was Christmas-themed.

"Thank you," I replied, making sure Miso couldn't wander very far in front of me. "We just have a few questions, if that's okay?"

"Yes, yes." She studied Cydney's collared shirt and slacks, hardly acknowledging that I was standing right next to him. "What is your name, son?" Mrs. Tankle used her display table of local arts and crafts at the front of the shop to hold her balance.

"Detective Keene, ma'am," Cydney firmly answered.

"Are you married?" Her eyes darted to the naked patch of skin on his ring finger.

"I'm sorry, how is that relevant?" Cydney crossed his arms, looking to me for an explanation.

"No, Mrs. Tankle, I believe he is single." I addressed the question for him. *And for good reason.*

"I can speak for myself," he muttered under his breath.

"Well, then." My eyes widened as I waited for him to respond.

"I am single," Cydney said to Mrs. Tankle.

"Delightful." Mrs. Tankle retreated to the cushy sofa that sat in the store's reading nook. One of her many patchwork quilts was draped across the arm. Mrs. Tankle quilted in her spare time, and she used her creations to brighten up the place. This week the quilt on the sofa looked like it was made from book covers—patches that mimicked the fronts of hardbacks in every color from apple red to forest green.

"Why is that delightful?" Cydney asked, leaning against a nearby bookshelf as if unsure of his own question.

"Because there are many fine, young, *single* women in this town, Detective Keene," Mrs. Tankle proudly responded, "and not nearly enough men."

I covered my mouth, noticing the change of color in Cydney's complexion. He took a deep breath, but the fresh air didn't help; he still blushed. Mrs. Tankle sat down and helped herself to an open container of shortbreads. She took her time eating the edges of her cookie before she popped the center into her mouth. She held out the container and offered us some. I shook my head and sat next to her. Miso sat at my feet, on his best behavior. He scanned the store up and down, and I prayed that if he spotted Mrs. Tankle's cat, he wouldn't bolt for her.

"Mrs. Tankle, I hear that you've entered the Sugar Mountain Bake-Off," I started.

"Oh, yes." She smiled. "Teddy came around last Wednesday and suggested that I enter my fruitcake recipe. I call it poor man's fruitcake. I use a lot of raisins, and a lot of spices. It never fails to impress. I think my fruitcake is good enough to receive an award, don't you?"

"Teddy?" Cydney cleared his throat.

"My husband," Mrs. Tankle clarified. "That's what I call him."

"And he is—"

"Dead," Mrs. Tankle responded bluntly, as if the word *dead* meant down the street getting coffee or reading upstairs in the den. "Anyway, I made a loaf this week with a can of fruit cocktail that has been sitting in my pantry, but I'm not sure if I made it too sweet. Teddy hates it when his bread is too sweet."

"Mrs. Tankle," I replied, trying not to stray too far from the subject, "did you know that Sarah Henson was supposed to be one of the judges?"

"I heard about poor Sarah," she answered. "Such a horrible fate."

"Is that what they're saying around town?" I asked, leaning in casually. Mrs. Tankle often smelled like cinnamon spice—the scented candle she kept next to her at the register.

"Yeah, what's the latest buzz?" Cydney chimed in. I frowned as I shot him a look. *Buzz?*

He shrugged.

"Oh, everyone's in a frenzy about the bake-off next weekend," she responded, taking a bite of another shortbread cookie. "Only one week left to practice...or protest."

"Protest?" My eyes went wide.

"Mim Duvall, of course." Mrs. Tankle rolled her eyes and grabbed another sweet. She popped the entire cookie into her mouth and chewed it in one big crunch. "You know, the pet groomer? I've always found her a bit odd."

Cydney cleared his throat, and I shot him a dirty look. I was sure that, to him, an outspoken pet groomer wasn't nearly as odd as an elderly woman who talked to her dead husband and had a cat named after a cherry. But I was also sure his definition of *odd* was different from mine. Just like his definition of *rude*.

"What is she protesting?" I asked.

"Word is, she tried to enter a recipe for dog treats, and the folks at Sugar Mountain wouldn't accept her submission. Apparently they told her the competition wasn't for canines." Mrs. Tankle chuckled, grabbing another shortbread cookie. She chewed it quickly this time, noticing that she'd eaten one more than she'd intended to.

"So she's protesting the contest?" I guessed.

"Uh-huh." Mrs. Tankle's mouth was full of crumbs. She munched like a haughty squirrel before closing the container of sweets.

"How?" Cydney was still standing in the corner of the room. As soon as he spoke, Miso jerked his head toward him and stared him down. "I mean, is she up at Sugar Mountain headquarters with a huge sign that says *dogs are people too*?" He grinned, scratching the side of his chin.

"Oh, she's been pestering Mr. Kentworth up at the resort to cancel the whole ordeal." Her response flew out of her mouth like a waterfall trickling down a wall of rocks. Cydney and I looked at each other. We hadn't spoken with Mr. Kentworth since his accident, and we still didn't know what had caused his accident, either.

"Now, that's something worth chatting about," Cydney muttered.

Miso jerked his head toward me as my phone buzzed in my pocket. I discreetly looked at the caller ID and all at once my entire chest froze as if a winter whirlwind had blasted through the store. I stood up, preparing to answer my phone somewhere more private.

"Excuse me, but I need to take this."

I led Miso toward the front of the Painted Deer Bookshop, staring at my blinking screen. Patrick. He hadn't called me since he'd left on his family trip to the south. I took a deep breath, making sure my back was facing Cydney in case he could read lips.

"Hi," I answered.

"Essie," Patrick replied. "It's good to hear your voice."

"How's your shoulder?" I placed a hand on my heart. It was beating so rapidly that Miso studied my expression with a critical eye.

"It's still healing nicely."

"And your mom?" I added.

"She's in good spirits," he responded. His voice softened. It always did when he mentioned his mother—a woman who truly had a heart of solid gold. "Being surrounded by her family helps."

"That's good to hear." I paused, hoping his reason for calling involved a return date for his little exploit.

"In fact, my aunt Clementine is planning on coming back home with us," Patrick continued. "I was wondering if you were free for dinner next week."

"Sure, I'm free." *That's if the killer doesn't strike again.*

"Perfect." His voice never failed to make me feel like a love-struck teenager all over again. I twirled a strand of my hair, wishing we were having this conversation face to face. Miso yanked me from my thoughts when he nudged my leg.

"Ah-hem." Cydney interrupted me by clearing his throat.

"Listen, I've got to go," I quickly said, ending our conversation. "I'll talk to you later."

"Stay warm," Patrick replied.

I hung up the phone and scowled at my so-called investigative partner. Cydney raised his eyebrows, glancing back at Mrs. Tankle, who had moved on to a brand new tin of ginger snaps. I took a few seconds to clear my thoughts. *Back to police mode.*

"You can't just get up and leave when you're in the middle of questioning someone," Cydney whispered.

"I'm allowed to take a personal call once in a while."

"Not when a murderer is running rampant through town," he retorted.

"Okay." I held up a hand. "Let me stop you there. First of all, stop exaggerating." Miso agreed with a short bark. "And second, you're just mad at me for leaving you alone with her."

The two of us snuck a quick look at Mrs. Tankle as she munched on a handful of cookies. She set a few down on her lap and called her feline companion. When Bing didn't respond, Mrs. Tankle took it a step further by scrunching her lips together and making kissing noises.

"Are we even sure that this cat of hers exists?" Cydney muttered.

"Cydney—"

Cydney interrupted me by clearing his throat again and puffing out his chest.

"Detective Keene," I corrected myself. "I know she seems a bit strange at times."

"An understatement," he butted in.

"*But*," I continued, "she really is a very nice lady once you get to know her, and she has given us some very useful information."

"I suppose," Cydney agreed.

"If you plan on hanging around Bison Creek much longer, you better get used to its little quirks." I waved goodbye to Mrs. Tankle and pushed open the shop door. The cool winter air immediately surrounded me.

"Well, if you insist." Cydney walked alongside me, but Miso forced his way in between us. "Where to next?"

"The busiest shop this time of day," I answered, looking straight ahead at the Bison Creek Bakery, where an angry customer was kicking a thick pile of snow like it was a Saturday morning ritual. Only on rare occasions did Doc Henry get so upset that he resorted to kicking the crap out of random objects.

"That's how I feel when they mess up my coffee order," Cydney commented, observing the doctor's erratic behavior. "What's his problem?"

The answer to that question wasn't so simple, but I had a guess. Doc Henry had been his usual self until a woman named Flossie had moved to town. I had yet to meet her, but I knew that she was an herbalist and she was stealing away some of the doctor's business.

But Doc Henry hadn't been shaken like this in the past. Many practitioners of alternative medicine had come and gone, so why was Flossie any different?

"Poor Doc," I said out loud. "I think he's finally lost it."

CHAPTER THIRTEEN

"Is this *really* about a cranberry scone?"

I watched as Doc Henry took a deep breath and tried to compose himself. A soggy bag of pastries lay at his feet. Cydney puffed out his chest, as he often did, making sure the doctor knew who he was speaking to. Miso stared the doctor down, keeping himself in the middle of us.

"It has nuts," Doc Henry responded. "Is it so hard to bake a scone without nuts?" He ran his fingers through his hair, a shade of white that matched the snow.

"Why don't we move this conversation to your office?" I suggested. I strolled farther down the street toward the doctor's office building, clutching tight to Miso's leash. The building was conveniently located just down the hill from the Pinecliffe Mountain Resort.

"What can I do for you two?" The doctor unlocked the door to his clinic with the soggy bag of cranberry scones in his hand. As soon as he entered his waiting room, he tossed the wet sack in the trash. Cydney crossed his arms, glancing around the medical suite. From the flat-screen television on the wall to the complimentary tea and coffee bar, Doc Henry's office was fit to accommodate VIPs. His regular receptionist, a not-so-friendly woman named Maggie, wasn't in for the day, but the lights above her desk had already been switched on. Ever since his wife had passed away, the doctor often spent the night in his office.

"We wanted to ask you a few questions about the Sugar Mountain Bake-Off." I started with the basics. Miso sniffed the floor, distracted by an unfamiliar scent. "I saw that you submitted a recipe."

"A wild plum cobbler I used to make for Clara," he responded. Cydney tilted his head. "My late wife."

"I see." Cydney nodded.

"We had a few fruit trees in our backyard," the doctor explained. "On Sundays I would pick a few things, usually plums, and make my famous cobbler. That was a long time ago. I haven't made it in years. A couple of neighbor kids tend to the fruit nowadays, but never mind that." He rested his hand on the receptionist's desk. "I would've thought you'd be more interested in what happened to Mr. Kentworth."

"You've heard from the hospital?" I responded.

"Please, take a seat." Doc Henry gestured to the sofa in the waiting room. Cydney and I sat down, making sure we were sitting as far away from each other as possible. Miso finally stopped sniffing, satisfied with waiting next to my feet. Cydney pulled a notebook from his coat pocket. He jotted down a few notes, leaning against the arm of the couch when I casually tried to read his writing.

The doctor sat in a chair opposite us. He rubbed his eyes and stared at the dry coffee machine. I took a deep breath and waited for Doc Henry to explain what he'd learned about Mr. Kentworth's accident. Judging by the fact that the doc was more preoccupied with brewing himself a morning cup of joe than he was with finishing his story, I assumed that my boss wasn't dead.

"He's okay, right?" I clasped my hands together, bracing myself for the news.

"Oh, he'll be fine," the doctor assured me. "It seems that Mr. Kentworth had been having dizzy spells for the past couple of days and, what do you know, he finally passed out while he was retrieving some things from his car."

"Well," Cydney chimed in, "that's a relief."

"Is it, Detective Keene?" Doc Henry clenched his jaw. "Because if Mr. Kentworth had only come to *me* first, I could've prevented the whole thing from happening."

"Do explain, sir." Cydney was ready to take notes.

"I can't give you all the specifics, but his medication was the root cause." The doctor shook his head. His cheeks gradually turned rosy, and they looked like two ripe cherries compared to the frosty color of his hair. Miso directed his attention at him, most likely sensing the tension in the room. The doctor rarely got angry. The last time I'd seen him like this was right before he'd fired his former receptionist—a young out-of-towner who'd insisted that a myocardial infarction and a heart attack were, in fact, *two* separate things. "Mr. Kentworth is on a couple of medications at the moment."

"So, that's it then," I stepped in. "There was a mix-up with the dosages."

Not likely on the doctor's end.

"I'm sorry, why exactly did we need to sit down for this information?" Cydney directed his question at me, which gave Doc Henry the fuel he needed to finally combust.

"You don't give homemade herbal concoctions to a man on blood thinners, Detective Keene," the doctor snapped at him. "It's common sense. I told that woman it was common sense, but of course she didn't listen to me. I'm just a medically trained professional, what do *I* know?" Doc Henry waved his hands in the air as he ranted on, naming all the things he disliked about Florence Wicks, aka Flossie the herbalist.

"Essie," Cydney whispered, "make it stop."

It would take more than a dish towel to soak up a raging river.

Miso barked, gaining the doctor's attention, but even that wasn't enough to pull him back to reason.

"And that name!" the doctor shouted. "*Flossie* this, and *Flossie* that. Her name's *Florence*, okay? F-l-o-r-e-n-c-e. Florence!"

"All right." I tried to keep my voice as calm as possible. "I understand, Doc. She gets under your skin. We've all met people like that." *Present company included.* "I'm sure she didn't give Mr. Kentworth those herbs to purposely harm him."

"No," Doc Henry admitted. "She's just ignorant. Utterly and completely ignorant!"

"There, you see?" I forced myself to smile, reaching down to scratch Miso's ears. "It was all just a misunderstanding." *Change the subject, Essie. Keep talking, and change the subject.* "Mim Duvall tried to enter dog treats into the bake-off, did you know that?"

Cydney glared at me.

"Essie," he huffed.

"What?" I shrugged. "I'm not violating protocol. I'm sure it's common knowledge by now." I paused, hoping I was right and that the thought of the judges biting into a bacon-flavored dog biscuit was enough to settle the storm in the waiting room.

"Indeed, it is," the doctor agreed. His voice had lowered to a more reasonable tone. "Of course, when I heard that, I wasn't surprised. Mim has always been quite the animal lover."

"Have you met her new business partner?" I asked, thinking back to my recent visit to Bone Appétit Pet Grooming.

"Oh, you mean…" Instead of saying the man's name, Doc Henry immediately pointed to his eye. Chip had been easier to get along with but, just like Mim, he too had his quirks. I recalled how the whites of his eyes were yellow, thanks to the fatty bumps that surrounded his irises.

"People call him Chip," I responded. "Nice guy."

"Strange name," Cydney added.

"It's a nickname." I rubbed the smooth coat of fur on Miso's back, and he finally relaxed again at my feet. My thoughts were on autoplay, remembering the chip in Chip's tooth and his admission that he'd once called Silverwood home. I hadn't seen his name on the list of Sugar Mountain Bake-Off entrants. Chip might have been the only one who wasn't planning on fighting for the coveted five-thousand-dollar prize.

"Fascinating scleras," the doctor chimed in. "It has been a very long time since I've seen a case of pinguecula."

"Ping-a-what?" Cydney leaned forward, ready to jot down the full definition in his notes.

"A more common name for it is surfer's eye." Doc Henry folded his arms, looking Cydney in the eyes when he spoke as he normally did when giving a detailed explanation. He was *mostly* back to his usual self. As long as there was no mention of lavender oil and reading auras. "It can manifest later in life due to the overexposure of the eyes to UV rays. You don't see it as much in these parts where the weather is cool most of the year."

"Shouldn't this fellow be wearing sunglasses, then?" Cydney's eyes darted from me to the doctor. He squinted, attempting to close his eyes halfway without actually fully closing them.

"Relax, Detective." Doc Henry chuckled. "It's not contagious. His previous profession probably required him to work outdoors. That's all. Back in my teenage years, the head lifeguard at my community swimming pool had it. He was a middle-aged man who had spent years and years working in the sun. My friends referred to him as *Lumpy*. 'There goes Lumpy the Lifeguard,' they would shout."

Cydney cracked a smile.

"We should probably get going," I interjected, checking the time on my cell phone. "Lots of work to do, right, Detective?"

Cydney nodded in agreement.

"Thank you, Doctor." Cydney reached out and shook his hand. "We will be in touch."

His manners are improving.

I nudged Miso and he followed me back into the crisp morning air. Cydney and I continued our stroll down Canyon Street, walking toward the Pinecliffe Mountain Resort. Cydney stopped to clear his lungs. He shook the freshly fallen snowflakes from his boots, stretching out his knee in the process.

"Have you ever had that thing looked at?" I commented.

"What are you talking about?"

"I'm talking about your limp," I replied. I led Miso closer to the mini hill that led up to the resort parking lot.

"I don't limp." Cydney stated it with such surety that I did a once-over of his bad leg.

"Yes, you do," I insisted. "It's hardly noticeable, but you do."

"It's my knee," he admitted. "It gives me trouble sometimes."

"Come on," I sighed. I avoided looking toward the creek that ran right into Lake Loxley as we passed it.

"Where are we going?" Cydney looked puzzled.

"We're going to the resort."

"Essie, we don't have time—"

"Trust me on this one," I went on, knowing that our chances of catching the mayor at home were slim. He was a man who always had a full schedule.

"But the mayor—"

"Relax," I responded. "It's Saturday morning. If Mayor Millbreck isn't on his way to meet his latest supporter for brunch at the resort, I'd be surprised."

"I hope you're right," Cydney muttered, popping his knee.

"Besides, Aggie makes a mean Denver omelet."

CHAPTER FOURTEEN

I snuck Miso through the employee entrance to the hotel, cringing when his collar jingled. Eli snuck up behind me, poking me in the side. Miso barked when I let out a loud yelp. Cydney observed Eli's appearance while keeping a straight face. His eyes narrowed at the way Eli's shirt was untucked, and his hair was messy like he had just rolled out of bed.

"Darn it, Eli!" I blurted out.

"There's no point sneaking around." Eli snickered, petting Miso. "The boss ain't here today, remember?"

"Shouldn't you be in the dining room taking orders or something?" I asked. "And run a comb through your hair. If my sister sees you like this, she'll iron your shirt for you. While you're still wearing it."

"Good point." Eli ran his fingers over the buttons of his shirt, attempting to smooth away the wrinkles. "When is she coming in today?"

"Not until later, I think."

"Right." Eli nodded, his gaze wandering to the man who was staring him down. "Is *he* okay?" Eli lowered his voice, acting as if Cydney couldn't hear our side conversation.

"Eli, is Mayor Millbreck around?" I ignored his question completely because the honest answer was deeply complicated.

"Haven't seen him," he confessed.

"He usually does brunch in the Aspen room, right?"

Eli did his best to ignore Cydney's hard stare, but it was difficult for him. His eyes jumped back and forth between me and Detective Keene like two tiny bouncy balls. Eli made another attempt at fixing his disheveled uniform.

"Yeah. I waited on him and the missus last week." Eli's eyes settled on Cydney again, and the way he had crossed his arms. Cydney's hands pushed out his biceps, which made his arms appear thicker than they actually were. "Is this guy going to arrest me or something?"

"Cydney." I nudged his shoulder, raising my eyebrows.

"Um, let me check on that reservation for you, Essie." Eli moved toward the nearest exit.

"Great, I'll be in the studio," I responded. "You know my extension."

Eli nodded and disappeared down the staff hallway.

"What was that about?" I asked Cydney with a roll of my eyes, starting our journey to the resort's private fitness studio by jogging up the first flight of stairs. Miso eagerly wagged his tail as he climbed with me.

"Nothing," Cydney muttered. The more stairs we climbed, the more Cydney cringed with every step. He was too proud to stop and take a break, but every time he lifted his leg he glanced down at it. By the time we reached the fitness studio, Cydney was casually rubbing his kneecap. It was obvious that his old injury had been giving him grief.

I passed the office, where Taryn was typing away on her computer, and headed straight for one of the equipment cupboards. I grabbed a roll of athletic tape and a small towel. I pointed to the nearest chair near the large windows overlooking Canyon Street, letting Miso off his leash so he could follow me.

"Sit," I instructed Cydney.

"Me or the dog?"

"You, Detective Keene," I insisted. "Sit down and roll up your pant leg."

"Am I allowed to ask why?" Cydney leaned against the opposite wall of the gym, refusing to walk any farther into the room.

"I'm going to ice and tape your knee. I've done it hundreds of times." I held out my hand like a patient mother beckoning her child to come closer. "Come on. It'll make your day a little easier. I promise."

Cydney scanned the room like the sheriff might be hiding in any corner.

"Will it take long?" He uncrossed his arms and took off his coat, warming up to the idea. I shook my head. "And you're sure it'll help?"

"It won't hurt," I answered.

He rubbed the edges of his kneecap as he decided.

"Fine." Cydney sighed. "What's the worst that could happen?"

"That's the spirit," I joked. Cydney took a seat next to me, but hesitated to roll up his pant leg. I reached for the loose fabric, but Cydney jerked his calf away from me.

"I'll do it. Thanks." He reluctantly rolled up his pant leg one strip at a time.

"Okay." I held my hands up. "I'll get some ice." Miso kept an eye on Cydney as I dashed to the fridge in the office. Taryn looked up at me. Her hair was pulled back in a tight ponytail, and streaks of blue were weaved into her dark locks.

"Hey, boss," Taryn greeted me. "You don't have any appointments this morning."

"I know." I opened the freezer and grabbed a Styrofoam cup that I'd previously filled with water.

"You stopped in for an ice massage?" Taryn glanced at the cup with a confused frown.

"It's not for me, it's for the new detective."

"What?" Taryn followed me back into the training room to get a good look. She stopped in the doorway as I examined Cydney's bare knee.

"Flex it for me, will you?" I watched as Cydney straightened his knee and bent it multiple times. Each time it made a faint popping noise. I studied the shape of his kneecap, noticing that it rotated slightly when he moved it. "Well, your patella is definitely twisted and irritating everything around it. Sit on the floor. A good ice massage should help."

Cydney exhaled loudly, but followed my advice. Miso sat next to him as if he too was receiving treatment. I placed a towel underneath Cydney's leg to make him more comfortable. Breaking off the edges of the Styrofoam cup, I placed the block of ice on the patch of skin underneath his kneecap.

"I've tried ice before," he mentioned. "It never works the way I want it to."

"Hold the end of the cup and rub the ice around your kneecap in circles," I instructed him.

"For how long?"

118

"Until the ice is gone," I replied. Cydney leaned in closer like he had heard me wrong.

"Come again?" He applied the ice directly to his skin, and began the process of icing his knee.

"When your skin is red, and your knee is numb, that's when you stop." I grinned, flicking a spot on his shin. "I should be able to do that to your knee, and you shouldn't be able to feel it."

"All right." Cydney grimaced, shaking his head. His opposite hand immediately covered his outer calf. An inked spot that, in his attempts to hide it, held my curiosity.

"What is—"

"I knew you would ask me that," he blurted out, "but it's nothing."

"It doesn't look like nothing." I scooted closer, trying to get a better look at it. "Is that a tattoo? Let me see."

It was apparent now why he had acted so weird when I'd asked him to roll up his pant leg. Cydney Keene didn't seem like the tattoo type, and I was very familiar with the tattoo type. My little sister, Joy, had talked about nothing else since she was fourteen, and at eighteen she'd fulfilled her dreams in one late-night girls' trip to Crystal City. But then again, I also had to admit that even the conservative could have me fooled. I was pretty sure that Mrs. Tankle had a string of nautical stars on her thigh.

"I was just a kid when I got it," he admitted, slowly removing his hand to reveal the black ink.

"A dreamcatcher?" Taryn had finally joined in the conversation. She walked forward, reserving her friendly smile for Miso. Cydney glanced up at her in her blue-streaked ponytail and gym clothes. I took a deep breath, expecting him to treat her the same way he did Eli—like she'd spray-painted the side of his car.

"That's right." Cydney's eyes locked with Taryn's. He spoke softly before clearing his throat and focusing all his attention on moving the ice block in perfect circles. His skin was already starting to turn pink from the cold.

"Can I ask what it means?" Taryn replied quietly. She too had lowered her voice.

"I got it to remind me of my father," Cydney answered. "He died when I was young, and my mom remarried."

"I'm sorry." Taryn took a step closer.

"Don't be." Cydney sat up straighter and stuck out his chest in a very subtle way. "I was practically a baby when it happened."

"So, did he appear to you in a dream or something?" Taryn bent down and studied the tattoo with a look of admiration on her face. Cydney paused, and his eyes wandered back and forth over the curves of her cheeks.

"No," he finally answered, pulling his eyes away. "Actually, he was Native American."

"Consider yourself lucky that you know anything about him at all," I added, running my fingers over Miso's midnight mane. There were times when I'd find myself gazing up at the snow-capped mountains wondering what my biological parents were doing, and if they were staring at the same bundle of peaks as I was. If either of them were even still alive. I jumped to my feet. "How's that knee feeling, Detective?"

"Starting to go numb already," he informed me.

"Good. When you're done I'll show you how to tape it for full knee support, but I recommend that you see a physical therapist."

"Doctor Essie at work," Taryn joked.

Miso scampered toward the office as the phone rang. I followed him, leaving Taryn and Cydney alone to get to know each other. I didn't know what type of woman Cydney usually went for, but it was obvious by the way his eyes had twinkled that he'd seen something he liked in Taryn.

A strange pairing.

"Hello?" I answered the phone in the office, ready to search through our appointment calendar for open spots. "Can I help you?"

"It's me, Eli."

"Oh." I waited for him to continue.

"I thought you might like to know that Aggie is throwing a fit down in the kitchen," he began.

"Did you eat all the leftover croissants again?" I rolled my eyes and glanced down at Miso, who was staring up at me with his bright eyes. "She likes to use those for bread pudding."

"No," Eli responded. "She prepped for the mayor's brunch, but he canceled."

I gripped the phone tighter.

"Did he say why?" I asked.

"No."

"Who exactly called in and canceled?" I questioned him further.

"The missus."

I hung up before Eli had time to go on. After our little talk yesterday it seemed that Martha was keeping the mayor far away from my stomping grounds. Maybe he really was guilty, and if so, maybe Martha thought that the whole *out of sight, out of mind* principle might apply in this situation.

Fat chance.

The mayor was still our strongest lead. He had been romantically involved with Sarah Henson, and if news of his affair were to spread through town, his reign as the mayor of Bison Creek might actually come to an end. For the last two elections, he hadn't had any competition. No one had bothered to run against him, and he always boasted that he was the only mayor in the state to be voted into office unanimously. Bison Creek was a small enough town, with lax enough laws and no term limits, that the era of the Millbrecks could last a very, very long time.

But the town's sudden rise in tourism had brought with it new political prospects.

Maybe that's what the mayor was afraid of.

* * *

The Millbrecks owned a house in the newer part of town. It was on the side of Pinecliffe Mountain where the majority of the local vacation lodges were located—the area of Bison Creek that was usually free of townies. Most of the permanent residents lived in the older part of town near Canyon Street.

"How's the knee?" I asked Cydney as the two of us pulled up next to the Millbrecks' house. It was easier to drive to their abode than it was to walk in the snow, and Cydney had kindly agreed to drive since my car was still dead.

"Much better," he admitted. When I had hung up the phone with Eli, I'd found Cydney and Taryn deep in conversation. I didn't have a clue what they talked about, but Cydney had been friendlier toward me ever since. The two of us stepped out of Cydney's car, and I grabbed Miso's leash.

The Millbrecks lived in a newly-built home made to look like an old-fashioned mountain lodge. There were tall windows overlooking the slopes, and a giant wooden deck that wrapped around the house, leading toward the backyard. The front door was framed with dark wood trim, and the stone steps leading toward the entrance matched the stone on the walls. Decorative rocks and rich green shrubs landscaped the yard.

Martha's monthly wreath hung on the door. Most people, my mother included, had wreaths for special occasions such as Thanksgiving or Christmas. Martha had a wreath for every month of the year. For February, the theme seemed to be all things red. It was decorated with bunches of berries. Some of them looked strangely real.

"Do you think they're even home?" Cydney muttered.

"We will soon find out." I shrugged, knocking on the door. I glanced down at Miso. If anyone could figure out if someone was inside the house, it was him. I instinctively let him off his leash so he could explore his surroundings. Miso immediately picked up a scent.

We waited a few minutes.

Silence.

"I have a bad feeling about this one." Cydney placed a hand on his stomach.

I knocked on the door again.

Still nothing.

Miso sniffed around the front deck, stopping when he came to a patio chair. Miso lifted his head, looking straight ahead of him, and took off running. His piercing bark echoed from the back of the house. My eyes went wide, as did Cydney's. The two of us didn't hesitate to follow. Cydney jumped ahead of me, his knee obviously a hundred times better than before.

My heart raced as I turned the corner and scanned the backyard. More patio furniture was arranged neatly on the back deck. Miso barked at a long wicker storage box that looked like it was big enough to hold a few collapsible lawn chairs. My stomach tied itself in knots as I approached it. My eyes darted to the back windows, and my chest froze when an upstairs curtain fluttered out of place.

I'm being watched.

Cydney ran to the storage box and lifted the lid. As soon as he did, he froze. I gulped, preparing myself for what I might find. My mind fixated on the worst possible thing. *Please, don't be a dead body. Anything but a dead body.*

I stood next to Cydney and looked down.

Miso continued to bark.

"You have got to be kidding me," I said out loud.

There was a body in there, all right.

But not a dead one.

CHAPTER FIFTEEN

"My wife is trying to kill me."

Mayor Millbreck had somehow squished himself into a piece of his backyard décor, and his pale cheeks were a dead giveaway that he was hiding from the worst—the wrath of Martha. My jaw hung open as I looked down at his shivering arms and legs.

"Come on, Herald," Cydney muttered, extending a helping hand. "Get out of there."

Miso sniffed the wicker storage box and barked.

"Keep that mutt of yours quiet," the mayor snapped. "If Martha—"

The back door flew open then, in one swift movement. Martha was dressed for a day out—slacks, a fancy blouse, and the jewelry to match. Her hair was a little messy, like she'd been out for a run, and the smile on her face was wide and toothy. The mayor hung his head, and my heart pounded when Martha glared at me first.

"Essie," Martha chimed, "come on in. You too, Cydney, dear." Her eyes darted to the long storage box on the deck. "You'll have to excuse my husband. He's a moron." She paused and took a deep breath. "Tea or coffee, anyone?"

"Um…" I looked at Cydney.

"Yes, thank you." Cydney nodded and followed Martha inside. Mayor Millbreck sat up, carefully lifting himself out of storage box. He stretched his back and shoved his hands into his pockets. Herald Millbreck was just as short as his wife. He normally carried himself with a superior sense of pride, but not today. Today I'd seen him at his ultimate low, and he looked nothing like the mighty mayor of Bison Creek that I was familiar with.

"Mayor, what is going on here?" I whispered.

"I should be asking you the same the question." He gazed at the snow-capped peaks in the distance, a beautiful backyard view. "Why did you bring Cydney to the house?"

"Because you weren't at the resort," I answered.

The mayor shook his head.

"All right, what is it that you want? Money? A letter of recommendation?"

"Answers," I replied. "For starters, where were you Monday night?"

"I was here with Martha." His voice didn't waver, even though I knew he was lying. Martha had been elsewhere on Monday.

"You're sure?" I raised my eyebrows, hinting that I knew a lot more than I was saying.

"Oh, Essie." He placed a hand on my shoulder like he was a concerned friend taking me under his wing. "Are you sure you know what you're doing here? I know Sheriff Williams thought it was a good idea to bring you aboard and all, but I don't think you know what you're dealing with. Police work is a tough business. Being well-liked by your neighbors isn't a good enough reason to work alongside someone like Detective Keene."

"What exactly are you saying, Mayor?" I took a step back, forcing his hand to drop back to his side.

"I'm saying you're not a detective," he answered plainly. "You're just a small-town girl who should stay in the tourism business." There was nothing threatening about the way he'd said it, but my cheeks still went fiery.

Was this his way of threatening me?

Attention to detail had saved me from a terrible fate in the past, and it was helping me get closer and closer to Sarah Henson's murderer. Yes, I'd been raised in Bison Creek like the majority of the locals, but that didn't mean I had nothing to offer my community. Mayor Millbreck studied me from head to toe, looking surprised when I didn't turn around to leave. Instead, I forced a fake smile just like Martha's.

I see now that she gets a lot of practice.

"I think I'll take that tea now," I said, stepping past him. Miso followed me inside. The jingling of his collar echoed down the hallway, grabbing the attention of Martha's Yorkshire terrier she called Peppermint.

The inside of the Millbrecks' home matched the outside. It had hardwood floors, a stone fireplace, and crown molding on the ceilings. I followed the sound of Cydney's voice to the kitchen. Cydney was sitting across from Martha at the kitchen table with a mug of coffee. Miso greeted Peppermint with a quick sniff.

"Peppermint," I commented, "at last we meet."

"This town has more dogs than people," Cydney commented.

"Oh, don't be silly," Martha replied. She rose from the table and snagged a jar of dog treats from the counter, shaking it to hold Peppermint's attention. Miso wagged his tail. "Little Peppermint here is the sweetest thing in my life right now. Aren't you, baby?" Martha did the same thing I'd always found myself doing when talking to Miso. Her voice went up an octave as if she were squeezing the cheeks of an infant. She gave both dogs a treat.

"Why don't we get down to the real reason we're here?" Cydney continued.

"I know why you're here." Martha avoided making any eye contact, and busied herself with straightening the assortment of jars on her kitchen counter.

"You do?" Cydney took a sip of his coffee, glancing toward the backyard. Mayor Millbreck was still outside. That was, if he hadn't made a run for it, but even so I doubted he would have gotten very far.

"I do." Martha cleared her throat. "I suppose Essie has informed you of my husband's insolence. Well, I'm afraid that's all the information you're going to get out of us."

"Is that what the two of you were fighting about?" I asked, scanning the kitchen for any signs of a raging argument. Nothing appeared to have been broken.

"Possibly," Martha replied, flicking a strand of hair over her shoulder. "We argue all the time. Herald hiding out in the yard like a coward is nothing new. Though I do enjoy it nowadays when our arguing escalates." She casually took her seat back at the kitchen table and swirled the hot liquid in her mug. "It means I get the whole house to myself."

"So you don't know where he was on Monday night?" Cydney clarified.

"I'll let him answer for himself." Martha rolled her eyes. "Herald! Herald, get in here!" Martha gripped the handle of her mug a little tighter. "He's probably eavesdropping by the door anyway."

It didn't take long for Mayor Millbreck to slink back inside. He held his head high, although his teeth were chattering from being in the cold for too long without a jacket. He looked straight forward with a twisted grin, but as soon as he saw his wife glaring back at him, he slumped his shoulders. Martha seemed to be the only one in town who could shake him.

"I was in Crystal City Monday night," he admitted. "There, I said it. I went to meet up with an old friend of mine. Dave Faumin. He'll confirm my story."

"I bet he will," Martha murmured.

"Don't start, Martha," he said through his teeth.

"Why, because we have company?" She picked up Peppermint, holding the tiny dog in her lap.

"This is not the appropriate place or time." Mayor Millbreck raised his voice the way he usually did when he bragged to newcomers about the countless times he'd beaten the mayor of Silverwood at golf.

"*Appropriate?*" Martha threw her head back and cackled. "*You* want to talk about what's *appropriate?*"

"Darling," the mayor interjected, clenching his jaw, "don't think I won't tell them your little secret as well."

"The joke's on you, Herald." Martha pursed her lips together as if she'd taken a bite of something sour. "Essie already knows."

Cydney wrinkled his nose, trying to follow along.

"Oh, she does, does she?" the mayor continued. "So you won't mind if I pop over to Betsy's salon and let slip that you've been sneaking off to the city to—"

"Herald!" Martha barked at him. She jumped to her feet. Peppermint skidded across the kitchen floor. "This is all *your* fault, and you know it!"

"I had nothing to do with it," he shouted back.

"Cydney, arrest him immediately." Martha pointed at her husband, her cheeks cherry red. Cydney put his hands in the air.

"Let's all just sit down and talk about this," Cydney suggested.

"You really should be arresting *her*." Mayor Millbreck pointed back at his angry wife. "You and I are blood, Cydney. You have no loyalties to that woman." The mayor scowled, eyeing Martha like she was a full-blown resident of Silverwood out to claim his title.

"Both of you, settle down." Cydney placed himself in between them. Miso hurried back, taking his stance in front of me as he studied the Millbrecks' faces.

Cydney lowered his hands, reaching inside his pocket as his phone buzzed. He answered it after glancing at the caller ID. Cydney nodded, saying hello to the sheriff. He looked at me, biting the corner of his lip. When he finally hung up, he headed toward the door.

"What is it?" I asked.

"We'll have to save this conversation for another time," Cydney said to the mayor. "In the meantime, try not to kill each other."

He walked briskly out the back door and onto the deck. I hurried to keep up with him, and Miso ran ahead. His paw prints made a path in the snow leading us back to Cydney's car. My stomach churned as I focused on the back of Cydney's coat. It wasn't like him to walk away in the middle of a questioning—the same thing he had scolded me for at Mrs. Tankle's bookshop. He had to have a good reason. A *deadly* reason.

"Get in." Cydney waited for me by his car.

"What's going on? What did the sheriff say?"

"He wants us back at the station immediately," Cydney answered. "The safe has been opened."

CHAPTER SIXTEEN

The fact that Sarah Henson had journals in her closet mapping out the day-to-day happenings of everyone in Bison Creek made my skin crawl. What made my skin crawl even more was that she hadn't locked those ticking time bombs away in her safe. Something else had been more important to her.

"Here you go, Doc." Sheriff Williams reached into the safe and handed the doctor a heavy object. He examined it closely. It was tall, shiny, and it had a rounded base that looked about six inches in diameter.

It was a trophy of some kind, and it could have been the murder weapon.

"Oh my," Doc Henry muttered, squinting his eyes.

"The safe is full of them," the sheriff replied, opening the heavy metal door even wider.

It appeared that Sarah's most prized possessions were her dogs and the various trophies they had won. And by the looks of it, her dogs had won quite a few. I scanned each trophy, searching for some sort of clue, but each looked similar to the one next to it. All of them were tall, shiny, and displayed golden, engraved plaques with Sarah Henson's name on them. Some even had the shape of her home state of Texas near her name. The safe couldn't have been another dead end; I was missing a piece to the puzzle.

I had to be.

"Do you think one of these was the murder weapon?" Murray commented. The reason for his absence this morning was obvious when he ran his fingers through his reddish hair. He'd taken the time to stare at his reflection in the frosted window, more than once. He'd gotten a haircut.

"No," Cydney immediately answered. "It's not likely that the killer opened the safe, used one of these trophies to murder the victim, and then ran all the way back to the victim's house in order to put it back again."

"He's right," I added. "Chances are, the killer still has the murder weapon. The killer stole one of these trophies. Maybe we can get records of Sarah Henson's competition history and figure out if a trophy is missing." But the evidence had answered that question for me as I observed each trophy in its place, noticing that there was extra space in the center of the safe. A spot reserved for the biggest prize of them all.

"That's a start." Cydney took a deep breath as he took a seat at his desk. I again let Miso off his leash, and he carefully sniffed around the police station. Sheriff Williams shot me a strange look. He wrinkled his nose, scratching the sides of his mustache as if he had an itch he couldn't satisfy.

"I see you two have worked out your differences," he observed.

I shrugged.

The thought hadn't crossed my mind, but Cydney hadn't irritated me since we'd gotten back from the mayor's house. He was growing on me, and it seemed that Bison Creek was growing on *him*. Or maybe he was working up the courage to ask for Taryn's number?

"For now," I teased.

Cydney grinned, reaching down to rub his taped-up kneecap. Sometimes the smallest of gestures was enough to create change. My first month living above the Painted Deer Bookshop wasn't the easiest. Mrs. Tankle wasn't used to having two tenants, or to the noises that two people could make while getting ready for work in the morning. I'd almost moved out because she'd made it a point, every time I walked down Canyon Street, to tell me I had lead feet. That all changed when I joined her book club, and committed to bringing an assorted veggie tray to the meeting each month, for the diabetics.

"Good," the sheriff continued. "Did you get an alibi from our *dearest* mayor?"

I locked eyes with Cydney, and all at once my mind jumped back to the Millbrecks' home. That place might have been pristine on the outside, but it was a train wreck on the inside. The Millbrecks' marriage was a whitehead waiting to pop—disgusting to look at, but you can't help it.

"We did," I responded. "But…" I stopped. Cydney had been dead set on clearing the mayor's name, but our visit to see him had been nothing short of shady.

"But we still need to make sure it's legit," Cydney went on. "I can do that, sir."

"Well done." The sheriff touched his breast pocket, where he usually kept his smokes. "And what about our other lead?"

"The bake-off?" I glanced at Doc Henry, who had paused to hear my response. "We've talked to a few of the entrants, but not many."

The doctor took a deep breath.

"Keep sniffing the trail. Opening the safe just confirms what I think we've known all along." He brushed his breast pocket a second time, his pinky finger twitching. "It explains the ripped pages in the journal, and it explains the missing trophy."

"Yeah," Murray butted in, occupied with the box of doughnuts on his desk. In the time we'd spent speculating, he'd been far, far away in Pastryland. "Wait...how did the killer get a trophy again?"

"We don't know for sure," I replied. The sheriff was too busy flaring his nostrils. He glared at his son, but Murray had no idea that his father was annoyed. He touched the top of every doughnut, making faint fingerprints in the glaze. When he finally settled on a chocolate one, he took a giant bite. Vanilla cream oozed out onto his chin.

The sheriff looked away and went on with his speech.

"Sarah either gave out the combination to someone or she opened the safe herself, which means—"

"She probably knew her murderer," Cydney finished.

* * *

After visiting most of the Sugar Mountain Bake-Off entrants, Cydney and I had learned one thing. Everyone wanted to win, and everyone was convinced they had the recipe to reign supreme. I crossed another Bison Creek resident off my list. Come next Saturday, this town would be flooded with sugary morsels. More than I'd be able to count.

But only one winner would be declared the sweetest of them all.

"That last lady didn't like me very much," Cydney commented, rubbing his hands together as a mountain breeze blasted through Canyon Street. Snowflakes covered our tracks, and the mountains surrounding the town were chalk white. The sun was hidden behind a cluster of clouds, and a blanket of fresh powder was spread through the streets. It was difficult not to squint when both the sky and the roads were the same brilliant shade of pearl. This was why carrying sunglasses in the winter was just as useful as carrying them in the summer. Of course, a dog like Miso with a coat that stuck out like a skunk in a candy shop didn't hurt either.

"Stella Binsby?" I grinned, remembering what Murray had said about her buying her produce from the next town over. Stella ran the corner market, and she hated to sugar-coat. She preferred her words sour.

"That's the one." Cydney kept his collar up to keep the winter wind from brushing across his neck. I tightened my scarf.

"Maybe you shouldn't have asked her if she ate a chocolate bar for lunch."

"How else would you explain that smudge on her face?" he protested.

"You can't tell the difference between a smear of chocolate and a freckle?"

"That thing was bigger than a freckle," Cydney argued.

"Fine." I shook my head, but Stella had it coming the moment she'd asked Cydney his views on nepotism. "It was a mole, but it wasn't that big."

"Let's agree to disagree." Cydney continued walking toward his car. "Who's next? Another bitter shopkeeper? A plumber with a pet moose?"

"Just one," I replied, "minus the submissions from Silverwood."

I looked down at the name. Flossie Wicks was a woman I hadn't had the pleasure of meeting. I'd heard good and bad things about her, and Doc Henry had blamed her for Mr. Kentworth's trip to the emergency room.

"Address?" Cydney asked.

"Another universe," I joked.

"Save the jokes for when we're indoors," he muttered.

I stopped. Flossie's brother Booney was responsible for running the *BC Gazette*. He single-handedly wrote the majority of the columns that appeared in the paper. I was surprised that Bison Creek still bothered printing a newspaper, but Booney had refused to let the tradition die. A few years ago he had an idea to revamp circulation by adding a section for town gossip. Mrs. Tankle, and even my mother, read it faithfully.

"If you were an herbalist-slash-professional-psychic, where would you be hanging out on a Saturday afternoon?" I asked.

"You must be referring to that woman who has the doctor under her spell." Cydney frowned. "Are you sure she's on the list too?"

I nodded.

"We can't avoid it any longer," I added. "Her name keeps popping up."

"Fine." Cydney looked up and down Canyon Street. His gaze wandered to the faint outline of mountains ahead of us. "She's probably in the forest somewhere chanting." He clenched his jaw.

"Don't knock it until you've tried it." I laughed, thinking back to my high school days. There'd been a girl my sophomore year who sold love spells from the girls' bathroom. Joy had bought one as a joke, and ended up using it on Wade even though the two of them were already together. *That one had backfired.*

"Isn't that her over there?" Cydney pointed down the street where a woman wearing tights and mid-calf boots was crossing the street. The woman shook the flakes of snow from her curly hair and glimpsed up at the second-story window above Morgan Antiques. That was Booney's office.

"Hey!" I shouted, jogging to catch her. "Excuse me, ma'am."

I held tight to Miso's leash. He barked, catching Flossie's attention. She turned and looked me up and down. Flossie smiled when she saw Miso, but the smile was quickly wiped from her face when Cydney caught up with me.

"Do I know you?" Flossie studied my face, narrowing her eyes when she came to my forehead as if attempting to read my thoughts. Flossie was an older woman with touches of gray in her hair. She was dressed in all black—boots that matched the color of Miso's fur, black tights, and a long coat that fell to her knees.

"No, but I know you," I replied.

"Afternoon," Cydney said, nodding.

"You have a very dark aura, young man." Flossie frowned as she took a step closer to him. Cydney glanced up and down the street before taking a small step backwards. "You two had better come inside. A storm's headed this way."

"A storm is *always* headed this way," Cydney pointed out, sounding somewhat annoyed.

"Aw yes, a skeptic." Flossie chuckled. "I can spot them from miles away, negative vibes and all."

"Excuse me?" Cydney crossed his arms.

"Mrs. Wicks—"

"*Miss*," Flossie interrupted me. "But just call me Flossie. I don't mind it."

"Flossie, we just have a few questions for you if that's okay?"

Flossie glanced at the office window above us.

"My brother is in one of his moods," she commented. "I can feel it. It'd be best if we talked somewhere else."

"How about the bakery?" I suggested. It was a short walk, and there was more than enough room for the three of us to snag a table in the back.

"I could do with a hot tea." Flossie's nose wrinkled when she smiled. She linked arms with me and began walking. Miso trotted happily alongside while Cydney trudged through the snow behind us.

"I see that you've entered the bake-off next Saturday," I commented.

"It seemed like the natural thing to do." She tucked a strand of gray hair behind her ear.

"Why is that?" I asked. A winter breeze brought the smell of fresh-baked pastries our way. My stomach growled. It was going to be hard to resist my sweet tooth once we sat down indoors.

"It'll give me a chance to mingle," Flossie responded. "You know, build up my clientele."

"From what I've seen, you've been doing just fine." I remembered her mysterious meeting with the sheriff. If Flossie could get through to Sheriff Williams, the most stubborn of them all, she could get through to just about anyone.

"Yes," she agreed, "but being well-booked and well-liked are two completely different things. I want to show this town that I'm not as strange as I might seem. I'm not a witch who is hiding her pointy hat."

The three of us crossed the street and entered the Bison Creek Bakery. There was a line leading up to the register, but the line wasn't as long as it was in the mornings. The aroma of baked goods enveloped every part of me. I took a whiff of the sugary scent, and let the warmth from the ovens thaw my fingers and toes.

Cydney grabbed an empty table as quickly as he could. I sat down next to him, holding Miso's leash tight against my side. As long as Ada didn't notice Miso was sitting quietly at my feet she would have nothing to complain about. Still standing, Flossie took her time reading the menu for the day. Her eyes scanned the list of specialty teas.

"Hmmm…" Flossie looked down and studied Cydney's firm expression. He wasn't smiling, but he wasn't frowning. He sat as stiff as a board in his seat. "Maybe I'll order a little later." Flossie sat down next to him. "May I see your hand, young man?"

Cydney raised his eyebrows.

"Here." I offered Flossie my palm before Cydney blurted out a rude response.

"Oh." Flossie accepted, studying the lines on my hands.

"Flossie, did you know a woman named Sarah Henson?"

"You mean the woman who was found frozen by Lake Loxley?" she responded.

"Yes."

"Not personally, no." Flossie kept her head down, her eyes glued to my palm.

"Do you happen to know who is judging the bake-off next week?" I continued.

"I don't pay much attention to those kinds of things." Flossie ran her fingers over the creases in my skin. She stopped suddenly, focusing on one in particular. "Oh, dear."

"What?"

Flossie let go of my hand.

"Uh…"

"What did you see?" I eagerly asked, my heart racing. *Is it Patrick? Please, don't say it's Patrick.*

"Something I haven't seen in a long time," she said in almost a whisper. I leaned toward her, doing my best to drown out the voices around me, including Ada shouting to her mom to bring out more almond croissants. "It's probably nothing."

"Great," Cydney chimed in. "Are we done here?"

"What your heart desires will require patience, young man." Flossie held up her hand and looked Cydney in the eyes. He lifted his chin, taking a deep breath. "And you, my girl, you are dangerously close to finding what you seek."

The murderer.

"You say that like it's a bad thing," I responded.

"Do you want to know what I saw?" Flossie cleared her throat. The pink in her cheeks faded, and her eyes went wide when she looked at me. Miso jumped to his feet, sensing the same eeriness that sent goosebumps up my arms. "Listen carefully. You will reconnect with someone from your past."

"That doesn't sound so bad." I attempted to lighten the mood, but the way Flossie looked at me still made my skin crawl. It was like she was digging into the far corners of my brain.

"To listen to this person would be unwise," she went on. "It will be the death of you."

Flossie had lied.

She was definitely some kind of witch.

CHAPTER SEVENTEEN

"The footprint was bigger than my face." Wade chomped on his vegetables. I saw bits of carrot rolling around in his mouth as he repeated his latest Sasquatch story from the silver mines.

"You couldn't have told me that *after* you swallowed your food?" Joy responded. She clenched her jaw, taking a sip of her water.

It had been a while since Joy and I had sat down together for Sunday night dinner. Naturally, Wade joined us at the table for our late-night feast of grilled veggies, potatoes, and half a pot roast Mrs. Tankle had brought me. Joy had come home late, having covered some of Mr. Kentworth's duties while he rested up for Monday morning. Wade worked at the abandoned silver mines in Pinecliffe Mountain, giving tours when the weather permitted and running the museum and gift shop next to the Bison Creek Railroad Station.

"That was the best part of the story." Wade shoved a wedge of potato in his mouth.

"That's what you and the Collins' boys do when you're bored?" Joy gulped down more water.

"The hunt for Bigfoot isn't a joke, babe. Old man Simpkins saw him once in this very town." Wade took a moment to swallow his food.

"Like fifty years ago," Joy argued.

"Does it matter *when* he was spotted?" Wade added. "The point is there's a gold mine strolling around these forests, and old man Simpkins is going to lead us right to him."

"Didn't old man Simpkins get so drunk last year that he exposed himself to half the town?" I said quietly, adding in my two cents. Joy giggled, covering her mouth with her hand.

"Haha, Essie." Wade stabbed a piece of his roast with a fork and popped it in his mouth. "I know what you're thinking, but he's a perfectly credible source."

"Sure he is, hon." Joy grabbed a napkin and lightly dabbed the corners of her cheeks. She was still wearing her work clothes—a slim pencil skirt and a cream-colored blouse. "And I suppose you think that whipping it out to pee in the street when it's below zero outside is *also* a good idea."

"Some people are immune to frostbite," I teased.

"You shouldn't believe all those rumors that Martha Millbreck spreads around," Wade replied. "Old man Simpkins did not get frostbite on his johnson."

"I think when the condition is minor it's actually called *frostnip*," Joy clarified.

I couldn't help but laugh. Miso stood next to me at the kitchen table wagging his tail and waiting for scraps. Joy had given in and had tossed him a few bites from her plate, which meant that he'd be hanging around the dinner table indefinitely.

"You two like to gang up on me on purpose." Wade narrowed his eyes, glaring at Joy and then me, his soon-to-be *reestablished* sister-in-law.

"How's the investigation going, Essie?" Joy used a steak knife to cut her meat into tiny, symmetrical squares.

"You can't ask her that," Wade chimed in. "She's probably not allowed to talk about it. Or are you?"

"It's going," I answered. The truth was that I was getting closer and closer to solving the riddle of Sarah Henson's suspicious death, but the investigation wasn't heading in the direction I'd thought it would. With the Millbrecks' alibis, the missing journal pages, and the victim's two prized Akitas still unaccounted for, I had no idea what wrench would be thrown at me next. That and what Flossie had said to me had been weighing on my mind. What did it mean, and was the visitor from my past that she'd referred to Patrick? She couldn't have meant Patrick.

"Well, I don't know if it helps you or not, but I still haven't found a replacement judge for the bake-off. There's absolutely no one in this town who doesn't have a close friend or family member participating. I'm considering taking my chances with a random draw from Silverwood. Mr. Kentworth would love that." Joy rolled her eyes. It was no secret that she was easily irritated. Being a hothead like my dad, she tended to focus on the downside of a situation rather than the upside.

"There might be another murder if you stoop that low," Wade said in between chews.

"What sort of grudge do *you* have against Silverwood?" I asked.

"This guy came into the shop once to ask for directions or something," Wade responded. "I don't know what he wanted exactly, but he was a total douche about it."

"And you're positive he was from Silverwood?" I reiterated.

Wade nodded, slurping down half of the water in his glass—a temporary alternative since we were out of beer.

"His shirt said Silverwood on it." Wade shrugged and picked at his vegetables.

I glanced toward the frosted window overlooking Canyon Street. The sky was a dark navy, and the glowing street lamps made the freshly fallen snow look glittery. My mind jumped back to a similar night when I'd strolled down Canyon Street with Patrick. The roads had been empty and snowflakes had covered our tracks, hiding us from the rest of the world. That was the night Patrick had kissed me. The night I'd decided that I wasn't going to interfere with what destiny had in store for him.

Maybe soon I would learn if destiny had brought us back together on purpose.

I was pulled from my thoughts when Miso hurried to the front door. He scratched at the wood, whining until he had my attention. I pushed my dinner plate aside and stood up to grab my coat. Joy and Wade carried on the conversation as if I was still sitting at the kitchen table.

"Don't mind me," I blurted out. "I'll take care of your dog for you."

"Thanks, sis." Joy brought a spoonful of vegetables to Wade's mouth. He grinned and accepted her motherly gesture. I didn't understand their relationship. Married or not, they were either arguing or making up. I zipped up my coat and stepped outside.

Miso trotted through the snow and out onto Canyon Street. Gentle snow flurries glided through the air right in front of me. It wasn't unusual for a light snowfall to pass through town at least once a day this time of year. The mountains needed it. The ski resort needed it.

I watched Miso as he sniffed along the snowy sidewalk, getting clumps of mountain powder in his fur. I chuckled when the pup glanced in my direction. He looked as if he had a pearly mustache. Miso sniffed some more, stopping directly in front of Mrs. Tankle's dark storefront. I placed my hands in my pockets and let my eyes wander down the street toward the Pinecliffe Mountain Resort. It was smaller than the usual hotel and ski resort, but it had brought this town big business lately.

Miso stopped his sniffing and growled the same way he had a couple of nights ago. His growl started off as a low rumbling noise in the back of his throat. Before I knew it, he was baring his teeth as if he was standing face to face with the fiercest animal in all the Rockies.

My heart pounded. I instinctively searched up and down Canyon Street expecting to see a shadowy figure in the distance. Not a single soul was in sight. The road was completely empty, yet the way Miso was growling like a wolf about to attack his prey made my head spin. I remembered the disappearing boot prints I'd seen last time this had happened. My eyes darted toward the sidewalk. The snow was falling just as briskly tonight.

The same boot print was etched into the snow, but this time something was different.

There was more than one set.

Miso continued growling, and I gulped.

There were clear footprints headed toward the resort, and next to them were *two* distinct sets of paw prints.

Miso yanked at his leash, pulling against my grip with all the strength he had. His leash slipped through my fingers like a stick of butter. Miso barked as he took off running. I sprinted after him, but I couldn't keep up. Miso's dark coat disappeared into the night, and all I had to go on was the sound of his barking. The barks grew more and more distant, but I kept running. My boots thudded deep into the fresh blanket of snow, a new layer of frost that had yet to be plowed.

I stopped to catch my breath, realizing that I'd followed Miso back to the scene of the crime. Only a small patch of land stood between me and the frozen Lake Loxley. I stood still, listening for another clue as to where Miso had gone. A winter breeze rustled through the trees, and the icy air made me shiver. My cheeks felt numb as I scanned up and down the shore, praying I wouldn't see the murderer's handiwork yet again.

"Miso," I said calmly.

CRUNCH.

I carefully looked over my shoulder as the sound of crunching ice echoed through my head. The muscles in my chest tightened. I held my fists out in front of me, clenching them as if I was ready to jab an attacker in the face. I wasn't going to end up like Sarah Henson, but the situation I'd been pushed into seemed bizarrely familiar. I was alone next to a frozen lake, and my dog had gone missing.

CRUNCH.

"Hello?" I shouted. It was the only thing I could think to do. I turned around, making a full circle. My eyes followed every shadow, and every swaying tree. The mountains looked like dark peaks in the distance and the moonlight bounced off the ice around Lake Loxley's shoreline. It was a mystical sight. One that I might've considered staring at for a while in order to clear my head.

CRUNCH.

I jerked my head to the side, observing a cluster of rocks and jagged boulders in the distance. The snow was clean around me, and the only footprints that existed were my own. I clenched my fists even tighter to stop them from shaking. *Maybe I'm going crazy.*

I took a deep breath and rubbed the tips of my ears. I was too cold to stand around waiting for the culprit to walk out into the open. If there was a culprit. I took one last look at Lake Loxley and began my walk back to Canyon Street. With any luck I'd be able to retrace Miso's paw prints and figure out where he might have gone. *Joy is going to freak.*

"Miso!" I shouted, heading toward the nearest street lamp. "Miso, here, boy!"

CRUNCH.

I stopped.

The noise was coming from behind me, and it made my blood run cold. It was the sound of ice crunching beneath a boot. I tightened my jaw, and prepared to face my stalker. *Please, be a deer. Please, be a deer.*

A sharp pain surged through my body, starting at the back of my head. I fell forward—a bed of snow beneath me waiting to break my fall. I didn't remember hitting the ground or being buried in snowflakes.

My world had gone black.

CHAPTER EIGHTEEN

"Where am I?"

My eyes opened slowly to a blank room. The walls were white, and the smell of rubbing alcohol was the first thing I noticed. I held my hands up in front of me. They were red and puffy. An IV had been attached to my arm and my vitals were being monitored.

"Rest up," a voice responded. A woman wearing scrubs stood at the end of my bed. "I'll let them know you're awake."

"What are you talking about?" I responded, trying to piece together why I was lying in what appeared to be a hospital bed.

The nurse rushed out of my room and quickly returned with a familiar face. Joy hurried to my bedside, observing the state of my hands and feet. The back of my head throbbed, momentarily taking me back to the last moment that remained clear in my head. The moment I'd heard crunching in the snow behind me.

"Don't worry, you still have a nose," Joy commented.

My eyes went wide. I reached for my nose, palpating every feature of my face.

"Joy, you'd better start talking."

"You're back to your usual self, I see," she continued.

"What day is it?" I asked.

"Monday." Joy glanced at her cell phone. "Barely Monday."

"Good." I breathed a sigh of relief. I hadn't been unconscious for too long. My back felt sore as I adjusted myself in my hospital bed. It was difficult to sit up straight without feeling dizzy, and my fingers and toes were tender to the touch.

"You could have died, you know." Joy nodded, wiping the smirk from her face. "Fortunately, we found you pretty quickly after you fell. You can thank Miso for that."

"Joy," I muttered, "I didn't fall."

"What do you mean?" Joy raised her eyebrows, studying the severity of my injuries. "You fell. It was freezing outside. You could have died right there in the snow from hypothermia. You're lucky you didn't get full-blown frostbite. Remember that hiker who got stuck near the summit last winter? That fella lost a couple of fingers."

"Listen to me carefully," I whispered, double checking that my room was empty. "Someone tried to kill me."

"That's always the story," she joked.

"Joy." I grabbed her hand. "Last night, Miso went running off again and I chased him. I followed him all the way to Lake Loxley, and then…" My jaw clenched.

"Yeah?" Joy urged me on.

"There was someone else there," I finished. "Someone was watching me. Watching and waiting. And then *smack*." My heart raced as if I were back at the lake, running for my life.

"You're positive?" Joy narrowed her eyes as she glanced into the hallway.

"One hundred percent," I assured her. "Whoever hit me over the head did the same thing to Sarah Henson, only she wasn't lucky enough to be found in time."

"Darn it," Joy murmured. "You're probably right."

"Where's Miso?" I asked.

"He's at the apartment." Joy took a deep breath. She was wearing the same outfit she'd been wearing the last time I saw her. "Wade took the morning off. I was going to also but—"

"There's too much to do for the bake-off," I butted in.

"Yep." Joy shrugged. "I'm glad you're okay, Essie. But maybe you should reconsider this little arrangement you've got going on with the sheriff."

"Sarah was a client of mine," I pointed out.

"I know, but…" She tilted her head, taking a moment to stare down at her high-heeled boots. "Is this about the money? Because if it is I won't move out."

"No, you and Wade need your space."

Lots and lots of space.

"I could move into his cabin for a while. It'd be free for me, and that way I could still cover my half of the rent until you figure something out."

"Joy," I responded, "I'm close. I'm really, really close to finding the killer. This just proves it."

"Aren't you scared?" Joy studied my expression, waiting for an answer. "The killer might try again."

Am I scared? It was a valid question, and the answer was an obvious *yes*. I didn't have a death wish, and I wasn't ready to die before my life had even started. I wanted to *live* more than anything, and that's why I'd accepted the sheriff's offer. I suppose it had turned into a way for me to help the town where I'd grown up. To save it from becoming a ghost town like many other mining towns had.

The residents of Bison Creek needed the Sugar Mountain Bake-Off to go smoothly on Saturday. It was good publicity, and it would keep a steady stream of business flowing into town. And most importantly, no one could know how Sarah Henson had really been spending her time. Her killer had to be caught so that her journals could be destroyed.

I took a second look at my hands. The cold had nipped at them, but they were still alive and with time the redness and the pain would be gone. I tried to clear my head, thinking back to the events of last night. The growling. The footprints. The *paw* prints. I locked eyes with Joy.

"I'm counting on it," I answered her.

*   *   *

I spent most of my Monday in the hospital, and Taryn insisted on covering for me at the gym until I was one hundred percent recovered. The truth was, I'd been as ready as ever to get back to work the moment I'd awakened with my head on a stiff hospital pillow and had traced Sarah's murder investigation up until now.

Carob and Cayenne, Sarah's prize-winning Akitas, were out there somewhere. But most importantly, they were alive. I eased my hands back into my regular cleaning routine. I practiced by washing the dishes Wade had left in the sink. The more I saw of that man, the more I understood why he drove my sister absolutely batty. Living with him was like living in a frat house. Just like Joy, he too had the habit of leaving his stuff scattered around the apartment. And Wade didn't even live there full time.

Miso rested his head on the kitchen floor, looking after me as I did my best to busy myself with housework. I had to come up with my next plan of action—planning each step very carefully now that the killer was after me.

A rough knock on the door sent my heart racing out of control. I tried to curb it with steady breaths as if I were sprinting on a treadmill. Miso rushed to the source first. He sniffed the tiny crack underneath the door that I'd stuffed with a hand towel to keep the cold out. Mrs. Tankle had yet to have it fixed. Miso looked to me, wagging his tail.

"All clear?" I said out loud. It was a relief that he wasn't growling. I peered through the peephole and saw a face that made me wrinkle my nose. I pulled the front door open, holding out my foot to keep Miso from darting outside. "Cydney?"

"Essie." Cydney nodded and stepped inside my apartment. It felt strange to see him in my living room, and it felt even stranger to watch him study every piece of furniture like I was hoarding a fugitive between the couch cushions.

"What's wrong?" I asked.

"What makes you think something's wrong?" he automatically replied. He shut the door behind him, brushing snowflakes from his shoulders. Miso sniffed his boots and gave him his stamp of approval by sitting and waiting patiently for a friendly scratch behind the ears. Cydney obliged, reaching down to pet the top of his head after discreetly rubbing his bad kneecap.

"You're here." I placed my hands on my hips.

"Aren't you supposed to be recovering from a blow to the head?" he snidely commented, rubbing his knee a second time. His eyes fixated on the open dishwasher in the kitchen.

"I'm fine," I responded. "I was actually planning on coming into the station later."

"That's a shame." He took a few steps toward the couch. His boots left a tiny puddle of water on the hardwood floor. "Murray was planning on serenading you, and bringing by a plate of his mom's infamous cabbage casserole."

"Wouldn't want to miss that," I joked.

Cydney's hand grazed his jacket pocket. He gulped, his expression softening.

"Essie, I did something I shouldn't have," he confessed.

He bit the inside of his cheek, and his chest puffed out as he inhaled. Only one thing could make him this stressed. He was a man of habit, and a man of the law. He had broken the rules. I didn't know whether to laugh or kick him out of my apartment and call the sheriff.

"Oh no," I breathed.

"I didn't know where else to go," he continued.

"Please, don't tell me you asked out Taryn." It was a lame attempt at cutting the tension in the air. Cydney glared at me.

"Why?" he blurted out, scratching the side of his head. His dark hair looked even darker when it was

156

damp from being outside in the snow. "Did she say something to you?"

For an expert investigator he wasn't very good at hiding his feelings for her.

"I'll give you one more chance to come clean." I raised my eyebrows the same way my mom had done to me many times. Most recently, when I'd showed up for a family dinner wearing a sweatshirt and yoga pants. Little had I known that my dad had invited over one of his *younger* male colleagues.

"I went back to the Millbrecks,'" he said. He cringed as he forced his hand into his pocket and pulled out a bundle of crinkled up papers.

"Are those—"

"Yes," he continued. He paused to clear his throat. A bead of sweat formed on his forehead. "At least, I think they are. I haven't looked at them yet."

"Cydney," I responded quietly, "do you realize what this means?"

The crinkled up pages were small, and the color of the paper was a faded beige like the journal pages in Sarah Henson's spy diaries. If Cydney had found the missing entries, then that meant that the mayor had been lying.

Mayor Millbreck was the killer.

It all added up. His motive was sitting right there in Cydney's hands.

"I hate it when you're right," Cydney stated, wiping his brow. "I really hate it when you're right."

"How did you get them?" I asked.

"I saw the mayor driving towards the freeway this morning," he admitted. "I went back to his house to see if I could squeeze more information out of Martha. I thought since she was upset with him she'd be willing to talk."

"And?"

"She wasn't home," he went on. "I went around back and checked the storage bin, just for peace of mind." He stopped and looked down at the pages in his hand. "The back door was unlocked. I thought maybe something was wrong."

"So you searched the house," I finished.

"I did." He held out the missing journal pages. "Here. I can't bring myself to read them. My mother is going to keel over when she finds out we have a killer in the family. She's a very strait-laced lady."

I could've guessed that.

"Why come to me? Why not go straight to Sheriff Williams?" I hesitated to accept his invitation to take the first look. The detective shrugged, glancing down at his knee. The one I'd taken the time to ice and tape. *The simplest of gestures.*

"As soon as I do that, he'll arrest him," Cydney replied. "I guess a part of me is still hoping that the mayor is innocent. Come on, Essie, just read it."

My hands shook slightly as I accepted the wrinkled up journal pages. They were as light as a flake of snow yet they weighed on my hand like a block of ice. I was moments away from solving a murder, and my heart pounded so loudly I was sure Cydney could hear it.

Cydney eagerly studied the look on my face as I smoothed the journal pages and observed Sarah Henson's loopy handwriting. The first page started with a date, and it was followed by the name *Herald Millbreck*. My eyes went wide as I read the rest.

A place.

A person.

An observation.

And a comment.

"Crap," I blurted out.

"It's bad, isn't it?" Cydney paced up and down my living room with Miso at his heels.

"I'm not sure if *bad* is the right word." I kept reading. Mayor Millbreck had a deep, dark secret, and Sarah Henson had cracked it right open. It was a secret that could end his career. For good.

"Is the mayor our guy?" Cydney asked.

"I don't know for sure, but he definitely has a secret worth killing for."

CHAPTER NINETEEN

I crossed my arms, dropping the missing journal pages on the kitchen table. Cydney stared out the frosted window, watching groups of tourists stroll the shops along Canyon Street. The things I had read were both shocking and strange. The mayor had been hiding something I would never have guessed. Not in a million years.

"I'm not sure how to say this," I began. "It's not the kind of thing that comes up in normal conversation."

"Essie." Cydney rolled his eyes. "Give it to me raw. No sugar-coating."

"Fine." I took a deep breath. "Let's start with the easy stuff." I flipped the page and stared at Martha's name. "Martha has been having an affair, and Sarah knew all about it. An account of her 'joy rides' in a black BMW are all right here."

"You don't seem surprised," Cydney commented.

"Well, that's not the weird part."

"Tell me the rest," Cydney responded. He said it as if it were more of a command than a hopeful request.

"The rest has to do with the mayor, and his…strange habits."

"How strange are we talking?" Cydney narrowed his eyes, hunting for clues as if they were hidden on my face.

"How familiar are you with fetishes?"

Cydney shrugged.

Oh snowballs, he's going to make me explain it.

"My Uncle Lenny once dated a woman who had to keep the volume on the TV at an even number."

"No, this isn't like that," I responded. "I'm talking about an actual fetish. You know, things people prefer in the bedroom."

"You mean the mayor has been—"

"Yeah," I interjected. "He's been hiring *ladies of the evening* for quite some time now."

"So, the two of them are doing some relational outsourcing." Cydney nodded. "That's not exactly information worth killing for." He nodded again, glancing up at the ceiling. He was rationalizing his way through the issue. "Okay, I can handle this. This isn't so bad."

"There's more," I added. The next bit of information was where the story took a freakish turn. "The women the mayor hires are expected to look a certain way. Or rather, *dress* a certain way."

"I'm not following you," he admitted. "Why does this matter? The mayor is tangled in a web of prostitution. Isn't that bad enough?" Cydney rubbed his eyes. He paused and counted as he took deep, calming breaths. *All this rule-breaking is going to give him a panic attack.*

"His reign as mayor will end," I responded. "But if anyone ever finds out that Herald Millbreck makes his hookers dress up in furry animal costumes, his political career altogether will go down the toilet. Plus, it'll be the subject of the *BC Gazette* for years. I, for one, don't want to read about that over a cup of morning tea."

"You're joking." Cydney studied my expression, his thick fingers scratching the tiny patch of stubble underneath his chin. A rare sight, seeing as he was always one hundred percent clean shaven. He really was losing his mind over this.

"No." I glanced at the clock on the wall. The one Wade had mentioned was a pointless addition to the décor because it didn't have numbers on it. It was already close to dinnertime, and the sky was white with scattered snow clouds. "The mayor must have broken into Sarah's house to make sure no one ever found these pages."

"But that would mean he knew they existed," Cydney commented.

"And you're forgetting the worst part." I gulped, letting my mind jump back to the state of Sarah Henson's closet. "Whoever broke into Sarah's house knew that she was out. Or knew that she was dead."

"Do you think it could have been Martha?" Cydney's eyes went wide. There was still a speck of hope in his pupils that his dear relatives, the very people who had urged him to move to Bison Creek in the first place, were innocent.

The facts weren't in his favor.

Someone had murdered Sarah Henson. Someone had broken into her house, stolen her two show dogs, read through her journals. The mayor needed one heck of an explanation to keep the sheriff from bringing him in. And given that Sheriff Williams and Mayor Millbreck weren't on the best of terms, it wouldn't have surprised me if the sheriff chose to handcuff him and parade his arrest through town for the fun of it.

"I don't think it was Martha who did the breaking and entering," I confessed.

"But you can't be sure of that." Cydney pointed to the front door. "Martha thought that the mayor and the victim were having an affair, but that's far from the actual truth. Maybe Martha broke into Sarah's house looking for evidence of the mayor's betrayal?"

"Why go through the effort if you are *also* having an affair?" I added. "Don't forget that Martha has been sneaking around, too."

"Just say that she did," Cydney speculated even further, "and instead she finds the journals."

"So then what?" I shrugged. "Martha murders her so-called friend because of her diligent note-taking? No. There's still something we're missing. Like why Sarah Henson was keeping those journals in the first place."

Cydney nodded and raced to the front door. He was prepared to leave just as quickly as he had arrived. I eyed my snow boots and winter coat, grabbing the wrinkled journal pages and sliding them into my pocket. I was supposed to be taking it easy, but I couldn't rest knowing that there was someone out there who wanted me dead. Again.

"Uh, where are you going?"

"To clear up this mess," he replied. Miso followed him to the door.

"Wait a second," I blurted out, grabbing Miso's leash. A blast of winter wind blew through the apartment as Cydney pulled open the door. "I'm coming with you."

"Essie—"

"Don't," I interrupted him. I gently touched the sore spot on the back of my head. My proof that I was onto something. "I always finish what I start. Whether you like it or not, I'm finishing this. I'm coming with you."

"Things could get ugly." Cydney discreetly patted the side of his hip—the spot where he concealed his firearm of choice. Except for the unfortunate events of last month, a weapon like that hadn't been drawn in Bison Creek for a long time.

"You wouldn't shoot your own blood, would you?" I laced up my boots as fast as I could. "I'm pretty sure there's a rule about that written somewhere."

"Very funny." Cydney frowned, but it wasn't enough to mask the tempest of frustration and paranoia roaring through his chest. His jaw was clenched and his pinky finger was twitching like the sheriff's did when he needed a smoke.

"By the way," I continued, "she's definitely into you."

"Who?"

"Taryn," I answered, though I was sure he knew exactly who I was referring to. Cydney ran his hand over his shiny forehead. "If I survive the next couple of days, I'm setting you two up." Cydney didn't object. Instead, he held his head high.

A date would do him good.

* * *

I sat in Cydney's car down the street from the Millbrecks' home. It was my first official stakeout, and Miso was so eager to do some more sniffing around that he started with Cydney's coat. Cydney patted Miso's head at first, but his patience disappeared as he wiped a blob of slobber from his sleeve.

"You really should think about crate training your dog," he commented. "Trust me, he would like it."

"I would, but he isn't exactly *my* dog to train." Though if I added up the amount of time we'd spent together, Miso was with me way more often than he was with Joy or Wade.

"Really?" Cydney raised his eyebrows. "He seems pretty attached to you."

I couldn't help but smile. I owed Miso much more than a spoonful of peanut butter and a belly rub. If it weren't for him, crazy barking and all, I might have frozen to death. In that moment at Lake Loxley, Miso was the only difference between Sarah Henson and me. I'd been minutes away from a similar fate.

"He's my sister's," I explained. "She and her boyfriend adopted him."

"And you do all the work?" Cydney chuckled. "I would've kicked them all out a long time ago."

"You don't have any siblings, do you?" I guessed. Cydney stayed silent. "I'd rather dog-sit than be completely alone because my only sister isn't speaking to me. It's a fair tradeoff for now."

"A glass-half-full kind of girl." He sighed. "I can see now why the sheriff was so insistent on working with you. He gets nothing but glares when he walks through town. Whoever heard of a sheriff with horrible people skills?"

"That's the question of the day," I muttered. "I guess that's where I come in."

"What's it like to live in one place your entire life?" Cydney asked, narrowing his eyes as if it were a trick question. I couldn't decide if he meant it in an admirable way or if he was criticizing my choice to stay and work in Bison Creek after college.

"I didn't live here during college," I corrected him.

"Sure, but you know what I mean." He paused, patting Miso's head while he waited for my response.

"It's both good and bad," I answered. "I care too much about this town, flaws and all."

"Have you ever thought about leaving?"

"Are you trying to get rid of me so you can take all the credit for solving the case?" I retaliated.

"You ask a lot of questions for someone with no police background." His eyes darted up and down the street as the headlights of an SUV came into view.

"I would say that curiosity never hurt anyone, but then I'd be lying." I grinned, observing the car down the street that was moving closer and closer to us. "I'm guessing you moved around a lot as a kid?"

"What makes you think that?"

"You noticed that I'm a Bison Creeker for life," I replied.

"Fine, I did move around a lot." Cydney watched as a car pulled into the Millbrecks' driveway. Their garage door opened slowly.

"Then you should know firsthand that people are never who they say they are half the time." I clung tightly to Miso's leash. "City or small town, it doesn't matter. You can find the same types of people everywhere."

"Hint received." Cydney shook his head. "I'll go easy on the Millbrecks."

"I was talking about the sheriff. I don't think he's the guy you think he is." For some reason the sheriff had taken a chance on me, and I was beginning to see that his stubbornness could be softened with time.

"Right." Cydney opened his car door, letting in a few wandering snowflakes. "That's why he's been seeing that crazy psychic lady and refusing to tell us why."

Before I could reason with him, Cydney jumped out of the car. I followed him, taking Miso along as we jogged down the street to the same spacious mountain home we'd visited recently. Though this time, the two of us had determined that we weren't leaving without answers. The holster on Cydney's hip would make sure of that.

Cydney pounded on the front door until Mayor Millbreck answered with a shocked expression. He straightened the collar of his dress shirt and glanced down the street toward his neighbor's house, not wanting to cause a scene.

"What's this about?" the mayor asked. Looking him in the eyes was like staring at Wade while he streaked down the hall because he was too lazy to throw on pants. I felt embarrassed. Like *I* was the one with a dirty secret to hide.

"We have some questions for you, Herald," Cydney responded. He was so distraught he couldn't even bring himself to call Mayor Millbreck by his proper title.

"I don't have time for this," the mayor answered, clasping his hands together.

"Make time." Cydney pushed his way inside.

I nodded, impressed that the mayor didn't hesitate. He stepped aside, glaring down at Miso as his paws tracked in snow. The mayor slammed the door shut and retreated to his office. Cydney followed him, making himself comfortable on the chair opposite the mayor's desk.

"You have exactly two minutes to explain what you're doing here or—"

"Or what?" Cydney interrupted. He was back to his *Detective Stickler* persona—the man I'd first met at the scene of the crime. He stuck out his chest with confidence, pulling a notebook from his jacket pocket. "You'll call the police?"

"Make it quick, Keene." Mayor Millbreck rolled his eyes as if our attempts to squeeze the truth out of him were extremely childish. The bead of sweat on his forehead said otherwise.

"This is how it's going to go," Cydney said casually. "You're going to confess to everything, and when I bring you into the station I'll let you keep what little dignity you have left."

"Excuse me?" Mayor Millbreck stood his ground, exercising the bit of authority he did have. Cydney kept a blank expression on his face. His straightforward statement made him seem bold, but I knew better. On the inside, he was still the same man who had knocked on my apartment door in a panic. Inside, he was shouting at himself for honing in on the man who he should have been grateful to.

"You've been lying to us this whole time," Cydney went on, touching the holster on his hip. "We know it was you who broke into Sarah Henson's house."

"That's absurd!" the mayor shouted.

"We know you're aware of the lengthy collection of journals in her closet," Cydney said.

"The what?" Mayor Millbreck resorted to playing dumb. An obvious sign that he was nervous.

"Why, Herald?" Cydney glared at his target, but the mayor just glared back.

"Cydney found the missing pages," I confessed. I pulled them from my pocket and held them high so he could see that I wasn't making it up. "We know about the affairs, and—"

"Stop." The mayor immediately cut me off.

"*Essie*," Cydney said under his breath.

I shrugged. "What? I don't want to be here all night, do you?"

Miso barked, agreeing with me.

"How much will it take for you two to keep your mouths shut?" the mayor continued, opening his desk drawer. His eyes fixated on the journal pages like they were a bomb waiting to blow us all to pieces. "I'll also be wanting those pages back."

"The truth would suffice," Cydney fearlessly announced, "and those pages are now part of a murder investigation."

The mayor clenched his jaw.

"I take it you think that *I* murdered Sarah Henson?" he questioned the two of us. "Well, I didn't!" Mayor Millbreck banged his fist on his desk to emphasize his point.

"Then who did?" I threw the question up in the air in hopes that an answer might magically come to me.

"How should I know?" The mayor wrinkled his nose. "That's not my job. Now, give me back those pages." His cheeks looked like two vibrant apples, round and red.

"Listen, Mayor," I replied, "you're in a sticky position here, but let me spell it out for you. You tell us what you know, and I promise that an account of all your freakish trips to the whorehouse doesn't get passed around the Grizzly at happy hour tonight."

Cydney raised his eyebrows, looking me up and down like he was meeting me for the first time. Miso barked, adding in his two cents. I guess Cydney's boldness was starting to rub off on me. Boldness…or rudeness.

"It seems that I have no choice in the matter," the mayor muttered. "I knew this would come back to haunt me one day. Have a seat."

I followed his instructions and dropped into the nearest chair. Miso rested at my feet, and Mayor Millbreck loosened the top button of his shirt like it was beginning to cut off his air supply. He took a minute to crack his knuckles, as if preparing his fingers for a write-a-thon. He gently shook his head and glanced up at the ceiling—a light beige that matched the walls in his office. The room was plain and boring, unlike the rest of the house. It must have been a Martha-free zone because there was almost no color or designer pieces decorating the space.

"Start at the beginning," I suggested. "And speak slowly because I'm just a small-town girl who should stick to tourism, remember?" I bit the side of my lip, my heart racing for blurting out yet another snide remark.

"This never leaves my office," the mayor said, staring at the evidence in my hand rather than at me. "When Sarah first moved to Bison Creek about ten years ago, I ran a background check on her." He waved his hands in the air. "I know it was wrong, and I'm not proud of it. But she sank her claws into Charlie Henson almost immediately, and I couldn't help myself. Charlie wasn't exactly what you would call a looker. I was suspicious."

"I take it you found a little tidbit," I added.

"Yes." The mayor took a deep breath. "Turns out Sarah had undergone a name change before she moved into town. I did some more digging, but everything about her previous life had been wiped clean, so I confronted her about it. I didn't want some no-name ruffian coming in here and corrupting our way of life."

"Because old man Simpkins swatting school kids with a broom for looking at his lawn is something to be cherished," I mumbled.

"Sarah sold me some sob story about how she was once a respected member of the dog show community," the mayor continued. "She said she came here to start over." He rubbed his shiny forehead. "The mayor of Silverwood was giving me some grief at the time, saying he was going to fix my next election and send in one of his own to take over, so I made Sarah a deal. I promised her I'd keep my mouth shut about her past if she did me a favor."

"By *favor*, do you mean—"

"No," Mayor Millbreck snapped at me. "I didn't ask her for *that* sort of favor. I asked her to…I asked her to…"

"Spy on us all?" I said for him. "Dig into all of our personal lives?"

"Her assignment started out small," he went on. "I had her track a few friends just to make sure they weren't in league with my enemies in Silverwood. Pretty soon she had set up a whole system, and began presenting me with heaps of information. She even knew about Martha before I had the slightest clue that my own wife was sneaking around with another man."

"She figured you out too, didn't she?" I tapped my foot, thinking one step ahead of him. I had a guess as to what had happened next. At one point, Sarah Henson had been the most powerful woman in Bison Creek and I'd had no idea.

"Of course," the mayor admitted, the tone of his voice curdling like a splash of expired milk. "She tracked my *habits* for months before she decided to use the information against me. I still remember the day she barged in here, journal in hand, demanding that I step down as mayor."

"So she threatened you?" Cydney clarified. He raised his eyebrows. The evidence being presented wasn't exactly stacked in Mayor Millbreck's favor. He'd had every reason to get rid of Sarah Henson, especially after he'd learned that she'd written down everything she'd observed. *Everything*.

"She did," the mayor admitted. He paused, tugging at his shirt like it was slowly squeezing him around the middle. "I told her I would do it if, and only if, she destroyed those blasted journals and stopped tracking the good folks of Bison Creek." He sighed, and shook his head. "It was a lie, of course, but I knew Sarah wouldn't be able to give up her spying game. She had such a wealth of knowledge at her fingertips."

"Why don't you just skip to the part where you arranged to keep her silent?" I asked, hoping that it might trigger a burst of truth. The mayor glared at me.

"I did *not* kill her," he firmly stated.

"No, you just broke into her house."

"I had no choice," he blurted out.

Cydney's eyes went wider than two mini pumpkin pies. He jotted a few things down, inching forward in his seat. The mayor's admission to breaking and entering meant that Cydney had the right to follow protocol. His favorite thing to do.

"Why risk all that and only steal certain pages?" The truth was out, and I had a small window of opportunity to collect more of what had really happened that night. It was like what Joy always said to my mom after being caught in a lie. It's easier to confess once than it is twice.

Maybe the mayor will spill the rest.

"Fine," the mayor muttered, rolling his eyes. "There were too many of them, and there was no time. Sarah came home early, and she had someone with her. Those two dogs of hers would've sniffed me out in a heartbeat if I had stayed."

"Who was with her?" I asked.

"No idea." Mayor Millbreck shrugged. "I was out of there in a flash. I came home, hid the pages, drove to Crystal City, and next thing I know, I hear about the murder. But that's not the worst of it."

Cydney and I glanced at each other. Miso narrowed his eyes as he studied a shadow in the doorway. My heart jumped as the figure emerged. Martha Millbreck had her head held high, and a twisted smirk on her face.

At our last training session, Martha had confessed to me that her husband and Sarah Henson had been having an affair. I guessed she hadn't figured out the real reason the two of them had been secretly meeting up. Until now.

"Martha," the mayor gulped. "Sweetheart. Darling. Honey Pie—"

"Herald!" she shouted, waving her hand in the air like she was attempting to swat a fly. "What is the matter with you? I thought we agreed you were going to keep quiet about those filthy journal pages?"

"Yes, but—"

"Need I remind you that you wouldn't even be sitting in that chair if it weren't for me?" Martha barked at him. "After all I've done for you, you repay me by blabbing your nasty little fetish to the police department?"

The mayor's entire face turned scarlet.

Being charged with breaking and entering was the least of his worries now that his wife knew the truth. I tightened my grip on Miso's leash and slowly stood up. Cydney followed my lead, staring in awe at the look of disdain on Martha's face, as if she were a mythical she-monster.

"Not again, Honey Pie," the mayor said softly. "We talked about all this."

Yeah, and look what good that did you.

I rewound my thoughts to the moment I saw him curled up in a storage bin on his back porch—a measly effort to ditch the scorn of his fire-breathing spouse. I couldn't help but grin. The universe had a funny way of serving justice sometimes.

CHAPTER TWENTY

"I'd love to be a fly on the wall during that conversation." Murray sported his new hairstyle—a shorter, neater version of the old one. He clasped his hands together, chuckling as he leaned back in his chair. A half-eaten doughnut from the Bison Creek Bakery sat on top of his latest paperwork. "Wait, how long do flies live? Maybe I don't want to be a fly on the wall." His mouth hung open as he reconsidered his comment.

"You could be a dog," I suggested, playing along with his proposed pseudo-scenario. "A Yorkie, to be exact. Martha has a little Yorkie named Peppermint."

"Oh, she does." Murray smiled, displaying his larger-than-average two front teeth. "That's right. I forgot all about Peppermint. Martha hardly ever takes her out."

Cydney and I had raced to the station as soon as we'd left the Millbrecks' house. Sheriff Williams had been shocked to see me waltzing through the front door, but he'd assumed I had a good reason for being out of bed when I was supposed to be recovering from my "accident" at Lake Loxley.

"Breaking and entering, huh?" The sheriff rubbed his mustache. "That little weasel. You know, just last year he had the nerve to offer *me* marriage advice."

"Can we focus on what's really important here?" Cydney chimed in. Still upset that his own flesh had stooped as low as breaking the law, he'd let me do most of the talking. I'd kept the details of Mayor Millbreck's exploits very brief because I knew Murray would ask a boatload of uncomfortable questions if I'd given him enough time to figure out what I'd really meant by *the mayor plays dress-up*.

"Yes," the sheriff agreed. "The Sugar Mountain Bake-Off is this weekend, and I won't have a menace running through the streets again when the press arrives. This person has already made an attempt on Essie's life. Who knows what else the killer has planned."

I gently patted the back of my head. The pain was strong enough that I cringed, but reminding myself what was there forced me to see what was at stake.

The bake-off.

The town.

My life.

For once, I felt like we were all on the same page.

"Sir, I suggest we set up a night watch on Canyon Street. Maybe we can even locate those missing dogs." Cydney read each item off his notepad.

"Does everyone agree with that?" Sheriff Williams looked to me immediately. I nodded. "Good."

Miso nudged my leg, and I leaned down to scratch beneath his ears. Unlike the rest of us, Miso knew who the killer was. He may or may not have known what the killer looked like, but he knew what the killer smelled like. *If only pups could talk.*

My phone buzzed in my pocket, and I automatically imagined Joy in a panic at the apartment because I wasn't in my room as promised. I grabbed my phone and stepped aside toward the front door of the station. I almost choked when I saw the name on my caller ID.

"Patrick." I answered the call on the second ring. A little too soon.

"Essie, I was hoping I'd catch you." His voice lit a fire in my chest. It had a way of doing that no matter the temperature outside. "I'm coming home early."

"Is everything okay?"

"Yes, everything's fine. It's just Mom. All the company has been a bit overwhelming for her. Besides, my aunt really wants to meet you. Are you still free for dinner this week?"

"Yes," I blurted out. "Yes, of course I am. When?"

"Tomorrow night."

My stomach did a somersault, and Miso studied my expression very carefully. Though the clock was ticking on Sarah Henson's murder investigation, I couldn't just say no. I didn't want to either. I'd been waiting far too long to see what the two of us really had after all these years.

"I'll be there," I responded.

Only a dog-napping assassin can keep me away.

CHAPTER TWENTY-ONE

Cydney was pulling an all-nighter, stalking the streets around town, while I was staring nervously at the Jayes' doorbell. It had been over ten years since I'd been on their front porch, but Patrick's mother still had the same wooden sign hanging on the door—a wooden letter J she'd painted red to match her flower boxes.

My stomach was uneasy—bubbling and churning like it was being stirred on a hot stove. I loosened the scarf around my neck. It was the product of Joy's one and only attempt at knitting. She'd taken up the hobby right after her first major split with Wade, but she quickly resorted to more thrilling methods of drowning her sorrows, as she'd put it. Ones that'd led to the sleeve of tattoos on her left arm.

The last time I'd visited the Jayes, I was thirty pounds heavier with frizzy hair and a thing for cupcake-flavored lip gloss. I was a different person on the outside, and years later I thought I was a different person on the inside, too. But as soon as Patrick had strolled back into my life again I'd slowly realized that I might've been wrong. Patrick still made me nervous. Even now that the two of us were finally going to give our relationship a go.

I took a deep breath and rang the doorbell. The door swung open immediately, a glowing warmth coming from the hearth in the family room. A large woman wrapped her arms around me, engulfing me in a cloud of floral perfume.

"You must be Essie." The woman's face reminded me of Patrick's mother, Anne, and so did her accent. Her face was fuller than her sister's, but her smile was just as sweet. "I'm Clementine, the aunt Patrick never talks about."

"Oh, come on, Auntie." Patrick joined her at the door, his face lighting up when he saw me. My heart pounded as he too wrapped his good arm around me. He was still using a sling to stabilize his healing shoulder. I took a deep breath, inhaling the scent of his cologne along with the smell of burning firewood. "I'm glad you could make it, Essie."

The Jaye house was modest, but it oozed southern charm at the same time. The walls were a warm golden color that reminded me of crème brûlée, and were covered with family photos. Most of them were of Patrick's various snowboarding competitions. Mrs. Jaye had even framed copies of all the magazines in which Patrick had made an appearance on the cover.

"And miss out on your mom's cooking?" I responded. "Not a chance."

"So, tell me about work, and—"

"Patrick, please," his aunt interrupted. "No business talk." Clementine was wearing an outfit suited for warmer weather. A flowing tangerine skirt fell to her knees, and it definitely lived up to her fruit-filled name. She was wearing matching earrings that were an equally vibrant color, but her attire had been dampened with thermal socks and a thick, wool sweater. "Come, we're almost ready to eat."

I glanced back at Patrick as his Aunt Clementine pulled me toward the kitchen. I was surprised to see that the Jayes still had the same water-stained, multicolored wooden table that I remembered spilling hot spaghetti sauce on.

Right away I noticed a platter of something chocolaty on the kitchen counter. Anne might've been ill, but she'd soldiered through a batch of her famous Mississippi Mud Bites. It was her specialty, a brownie-like bar she used to make with her mother every Sunday.

"Those things should be in a lockbox," I muttered.

"Aren't they amazing?" Clementine helped herself to a piece. "I have to admit, my big sister inherited our mother's baking gene. Unfortunately, it seems that it only passed on to *one* of her children."

Patrick joined the two of us in the kitchen. His wavy locks shone golden in the light, and the color of his winter sweater matched the hazel in his eyes. For a brief moment our eyes locked, and I thought of the last time we'd seen each other. The last time we'd touched. Being back at the Jayes' was more than just a nostalgic trip down memory lane. It felt like home.

"I'm sure that's not true," I answered, keeping an eye on Patrick as he walked past me, gently brushing his elbow against mine.

"It is, honey." Clementine ate her second morsel of dessert just as easily as she'd eaten the first. She didn't even have to think about it. "Annie Mae has walked me through the recipe dozens of times and mine never come out as good as hers."

"Annie Mae?" As soon as I repeated the name back to myself, I smiled. Patrick's mother hadn't started going by Anne until she'd moved to Bison Creek. I guess she figured she stood out enough with her homemade sweet tea and her southern accent.

"Habit." Clementine giggled to herself. "I've been calling my sister Annie Mae my whole life. I always forget that she goes by Anne nowadays."

"And Clementine?"

"Is my name through and through," she finished, nibbling on a third chocolate square. "Of course, you're welcome to call me Tine-Tine like Patrick did when he was little."

"Pretty impressive for a two-year-old, you have to admit," he added.

"Auntie's little show-off," she joked. "I take it Patrick has told you the good news?" She paused, waiting for me to respond, but I had no clue what she was talking about. *Good news? I could use some good news.*

"No, he hasn't."

"Shame on you." Clementine shook her head. Her hair was wavy like Patrick's, but it was a medium shade of brown, a color that reminded me of mocha—a drink I hadn't touched in a long time thanks to my caffeine-free New Year's resolution. So far I hadn't caved.

"I was going to tell her as soon as she got here," Patrick replied. "You beat me to it."

"I've decided to move in," she cheerily announced. "I hope this town welcomes newcomers with open arms because I plan on staying for a very long time. I might even convince my daughter and feisty little grandson to join me." Clementine clapped her hands together, licking her lips as if she'd saved a chunk of dessert in her mouth for just the right moment.

"Thanks to Patrick, I've just bought the old Weston house."

"Really." I glanced at Patrick, who knew as well as I did that the old Weston place had been abandoned since we were in high school. "Is that house even fit to live in?"

"Oh, honey, I'm not going to be living there," she assured me. "I'm turning it into a bed and breakfast."

The old Weston house had been built in the late 1800s by the Weston family. Not far from Canyon Street, it was a classic Queen Anne Victorian with all the trimmings. The Weston's were a wealthy family, and they'd owned a share of the silver mines in Pinecliffe Mountain. But after their only daughter had gone missing, Mr. and Mrs. Weston had let their gorgeous estate fall to pieces.

"That sounds like quite a project." I bit the corner of my cheek to keep myself from spouting off anything more. Like how old man Simpkins always spat when he walked past it, claiming it was cursed land.

"I'm aware of that," Clementine continued, "but this town is entering into a revival phase. I can feel it. I'm sure that, in time, I won't be the only new business around here. Besides, it was always the plan to live close to my dear sister and my *perfect* nephew." She reached for Patrick's cheeks like he was a rosy-faced toddler.

"I never know if she's being sarcastic or not," Patrick pointed out. "I'm going to go check on Mom." Patrick squeezed my arm as he left the kitchen, leaving me alone with his aunt.

"So." I broke the silence by mentioning the one thing every person I'd ever met had an opinion about. A boring yet surefire conversation starter. "How are you liking this winter weather?"

My dad had told me once that chatting about the upcoming forecast was a definite sign that you'd arrived at adulthood.

"Oh criminy, is it always this cold here?"

"It does clear up a bit during the summer months, although it did snow last July."

"Snow is something I'm just going to have to get used to," Clementine admitted. "I have to say, Essie, I'm glad I finally got to meet you. You're just as I pictured."

"How do you mean?" I crossed my arms, leaning against the kitchen counter so I couldn't see the plate of Mississippi Mud Bites that had been calling out to me. Anne's kitchen was cozy. There were hand-stitched curtains over the window above the sink—a beige fabric with red roosters. The kitchen cabinets had been painted white, and white jars with labels lined the countertop. She even kept one of the jars open to store her cooking utensils. A Sugar Mountain logo was stamped on most of the handles.

"Patrick has told me a lot about you. About how the two of you used to be good friends."

"We were kids, and we were neighbors." I shrugged, trying not to read into her comment. But if Patrick had mentioned our childhood, he might've also mentioned that I'd been twice my current size, and shier than a baby fox. "Our friendship was inevitable, I guess. Until we got to high school."

"I *was* talking about high school," she added.

"Oh."

The muscles in my torso flexed, tightening so that I started to feel a little breathless. *Snap out of it, Essie.* I had a job, an apartment, and a bad track record in the love department—I wasn't a kid anymore. Why was I so nervous? Why did I care what Clementine, a woman I barely knew, thought of me?

"Are you okay, dear? Can I get you a glass of water?" Clementine snagged a glass from the cupboard and filled it with cold water. "Here. This'll soothe your throat."

I touched the side of my face. It was feverishly warm, an outward expression of what was going on in my head. I took a few gulps, thinking of ways I could change the subject.

"Thanks," I said. "How is Mrs. Jaye doing?"

"She's hanging in there." The wide-eyed smile on Clementine's face slowly faded. "As she says every morning, she's taking it one day at a time. The treatment she'd been going through knocked the energy right out of her, but we're hopeful." The faint sparkle in her eye pulled me back to the moment when Patrick had first admitted to me that his mother had cancer. He too had a small glimmer of hope in his eyes, one that hadn't left. "I do wish that I could find something to brighten her spirits though. Baking seems to be helping, even though her taste buds seem to be shot right now."

"It's too bad you didn't arrive here sooner." I eyed the chocolaty squares that I'd once eaten a whole plate of, one very nauseous Christmas Eve many, many years ago. "You could've entered her Mud Bites in the Sugar Mountain Bake-Off. They'd win hands down."

Clementine raised her eyebrows, and she glared at the plate of baked goods on the counter like they were bars made of solid gold. She gently scratched the tip of her chin like she was attempting to solve a riddle.

"Essie, you've just solved all my problems. Is there *any* way we can still enter her recipe in the bake-off?"

We?

"I can ask my sister," I replied. "I know of at least one entry that won't be making it in." *Thank goodness for Mim and her dog treat revolt.* "But even if we could still enter her recipe, are you sure she'd be okay with it?"

Clementine cleared her throat, hesitating to give me a clear answer.

"Well, maybe we just won't tell her."

CHAPTER TWENTY-TWO

"You want me to what?"

Joy was lounging on the couch in a pair of fuzzy slipper socks while Wade had his usual evening beer with friends down at the Grizzly. I grinned, noticing that Joy and Miso were finally having some much needed bonding time. Maybe she really was more maternal than she'd thought. I searched for a clean mug for my evening teacap—the word Joy had made up for the cup of tea I used to wind down before bed.

"Please, it would mean so much to Mrs. Jaye," I responded. "At least, I think it would."

"The deadline has already passed," Joy answered. "I can't change the rules. I'm just the event planner."

"But you could slip an extra entry into the pile, right? I mean, it's just a recipe." I skimmed through my herbal tea selection. Since cutting out coffee, my tea supply had practically tripled. I now had everything from lemon ginger to chocolate tea.

"I suppose I could try it, but don't be bummed if it's tossed out." Joy turned to watch me in the kitchen. Since she'd gotten back together with Wade we'd barely spent any time together. Joy was the type of person who had to be forced to take vacations, and she'd been known to be up checking emails at 3 A.M. Tonight was a rare occurrence. "On second thought, we've had to make lots of last-minute changes so the judges might not even notice the recipe hasn't been reviewed yet."

"I take it you finally found a replacement judge?"

"Flossie," Joy answered. The name brought a sour taste to my mouth. Not because her natural remedies drove me crazy the way they had Doc Henry. It was the fortune-telling that had thrown me for a loop, and had made me question if Patrick and I were right for each other. *Don't leave it to Flossie to decide your fate.*

"Flossie? Really?"

"She hasn't lived here for years, and she's agreed to withdraw her entry just for the occasion." Joy laughed. "Plus, I think she put some kind of love spell on Mr. Kentworth. He insisted that we choose her as Sarah Henson's replacement."

"Interesting."

"Did I solve the case for you, Detective?" she joked.

"Hardly." I shook my head. "How's your latest project coming?" I said, grinning because I knew exactly how she would respond.

"Work or the boyfriend?" Joy grinned back as she rested her chin on the back of the couch.

"What's it like to rekindle a lost romance?" I joked. The odd poured bowl of cereal was as romantic as Wade got—his idea of breakfast in bed. He'd have burned the toast.

"I should be asking you the same question," she retorted. "What's this little surprise Patrick's been hiding, and has he even invited you up to his new place? I heard it has an entire room dedicated to his collection of vintage pinball machines."

"He hasn't told me yet." I sighed. "And believe me, I asked." I'd avoided the subject all through dinner even though it was at the forefront of my mind. I'd sat at the dinner table too nervous to eat much, but I forced as many mouthfuls of Anne's pot pie, made with Clementine's assistance, into my mouth. Anne's face had been gaunter than ever, and her already fragile frame had looked rail thin. I'd done my best not to stare at her with eyes as wide as powdered doughnut holes. I'd thought it best not to direct any extra attention at her.

"It's probably something stupid." Joy turned back toward the television and reclined sideways so that her feet crowded Miso. "Something like…he wants you to help him pick out furniture."

"Furniture-picking is actually a pretty big step," I argued. "It means he trusts my opinion, and he wants me to be comfortable at his place."

"What if he asks you to move in?" Joy tossed the idea out in the open, but the thought of moving in with Patrick made my stomach feel queasy. I continued prepping my nightly tea, and tried not think about sharing a bed with the man I'd had a crush on since grade school. At this point, a good night kiss was as far as we'd gotten due to Patrick's busy schedule. And hospital stay.

"He's not going to ask me that," I responded, semi-confident about my answer. I nodded, reminding myself that Patrick's parents were very religious. "Besides, I doubt his parents would approve unless we were married or engaged."

"He's a grown man."

"He's also terrified of disappointing his mother," I said, blowing on my tea.

"Maybe he's going to propose then," Joy suggested. My heart pounded, just thinking about it. Joy had been married once before, but even though I'd had serious boyfriends in the past I had yet to walk down the aisle. I couldn't even imagine what that must feel like. All I knew was that even daydreaming about it couldn't stop me from imagining all the things that could go wrong.

"No." I took a sip of my tea. It was still too hot. I rubbed my tongue over the roof of my mouth. I'd slightly burned it. "Absolutely not. He's not ready for that. Especially not after what happened with his ex."

"You've been on *one* date," Joy responded, "and you already know him that well?" She chuckled to herself. "I don't understand the two of you."

"Ditto." I raised my eyebrows. Joy's relationships sped along at over one hundred miles per hour. I couldn't live my life that way. So fast, and so carefree.

"Hey, Wade and I actually dated *all* through high school." She turned to look at me again, tossing a strand of hair over her shoulder. "I know him better than his own mother does."

"Do you know him well enough to get him to keep his pants on?" I teased her.

"I tried changing him once, sis. It didn't work." She rolled her eyes. "If there's one thing I've learned about relationships, it's that you can't change the other person no matter how hard you try."

"I know. I know." I sat at the kitchen table and attempted another sip of my steamy teacap. "I should accept people as they are. I get it."

"No," Joy replied, "men don't like it when you tell them what to do. It's best to make them think it was *their* idea."

"What would I do without your words of wisdom?"

"Hey, I'm just trying to help." She nodded at Miso and petted his shiny, black coat. "I've taken a new approach with Wade this time, and it seems to be working."

"Every time he washes a dish you give him a treat?" I guessed. I couldn't help myself from blurting out the first thoughts that came to my mind. Luckily, Joy was thick-skinned. And though she was a hothead, she always smiled when I slipped into my sparse moments of pessimism. They were normally brought on by an overload of stress. Or in this case, a blow to the head.

"Laugh all you want." Joy sat up straight with her hands clasped gently on her lap. "It works for dogs, and it works for men too. I'm taking my new relationship one trick at a time."

"What happens when Wade catches on?" I asked.

"He won't. All he cares about are the rewards."

"I'm not going to ask what those are," I mumbled.

Miso raised his head and trotted to the door. I set my cup of tea on the table and gulped. I'd promised myself that if Miso ever again begged to go outside only to growl at a faded set of footprints, I'd call

Cydney immediately. I'd also keep my head covered. It was still tender from the last time Sarah Henson's killer had gone on a rampage. My heart raced as Miso stared at the doorknob.

A loud knock made me jump. I placed a hand on my chest as Joy got up to answer it. She ran her fingers through her hair and glanced through the peephole. She looked in my direction and smirked.

"It's for you," Joy whispered. She cleared her throat and pulled the front door open. Miso wagged his tail as Patrick poked his head inside the apartment. "Patrick. Nice to see you."

"Hey, Joy," he responded. "Is your sister home?"

"Of course." Joy had a scarily perfect way of changing the tone of her voice on command. "Please, come in." It was like she had two personalities. There was business Joy who oozed professionalism and epitomized the phrase *all work and no play*. And then there was casual Joy—my sister. The woman who ironically never lived up to her name because she did far too much complaining.

Joy smiled at Patrick and waited for him to sit down. I cowered in a corner of the kitchen, checking my hair in my reflection on the microwave. Joy offered Patrick a drink before inching toward me with a twisted grin. She slyly pointed to her ring finger, implying that Patrick's special news was indeed a proposal—her way of making me blush.

"*Joy*," I muttered.

"I'll be in my room," she replied.

Miso escorted her to her bedroom before jogging back into the kitchen to retrieve me. I took a deep breath and walked into the family room. Patrick jumped to his feet. He was wearing a navy beanie to keep his head warm, and his ski coat was unzipped, accommodating his sling.

"Hi," I said.

"Hi." Patrick grinned, his hazel eyes glimmering.

"Um, what are you doing here? Did I leave something at your parents' house?"

"No," he responded automatically. "No, everyone had a really great time. My aunt said you were, and I quote, 'delightful company.'"

"Good."

"She said the two of you had plans on Saturday?" he continued.

"Oh, the Sugar Mountain Bake-Off at the resort," I clarified. "Most of the town will be there."

"Essie." Patrick paused, glancing down at his snow boots and at Miso waiting patiently for a friendly rub. "Look, I don't want to sound crazy, but—"

"Let me guess," I chimed in. "Through the foggy window in your bedroom you saw a familiar feline staring back at you." Patrick, being the superstitious man that he was, had a theory that his childhood cat, Snowflake, was still out there warning him when life took him down treacherous roads.

"You love bringing up Snowflake." He laughed, cutting some of the tension in the room. "No, I've been thinking a lot about something you said at dinner."

"I said a lot of things at dinner," I replied. "One of them being how I ate a chocolate-covered ant in our eighth grade science lab for extra credit when really I thought it was just a free piece of candy."

"Right." He inched close enough so that I could smell the spiciness of his cologne. He smelled like he'd sprayed some on his neck right before knocking on my door. "But I'm talking about what you said about how you settled down in Bison Creek after college, and you haven't regretted it once."

"Yeah."

"I did the opposite." He clenched his jaw, his eyes softening.

"I know," I answered.

"I regret it," he went on.

"But your career—"

"It means nothing if I have nowhere to belong," he finished.

I gulped. My chest pounded, and I gently touched my ring finger as I thought about what Joy had said. I knew Anne wanted to see her son happy, and I knew that Patrick wanted to make Bison Creek his new home. Did that new home include a doting wife? Was Patrick really thinking of proposing?

"I understand." My voice was wary, much like Joy when she balanced a tub of ice cream, a bowl, chocolate syrup, and a bag of cookies all in one hand so she'd only have to make one trip to the table.

"Which brings me to my next point," he went on, reaching for my hand. "I've been debating whether or not I should do this…but life's too short to sit around analyzing every little thing that could go wrong."

Don't I know it.

Miso let out an anxious bark followed by a bit of whining. I took a quick glimpse at Joy's bedroom door. It was cracked, and I was certain she was eavesdropping. My heart raced so fast that I felt dizzy from the storm cloud of thoughts circling my brain. *Is he or isn't he? What do I do? What do I say?*

"Patrick, what is it?" As soon as I asked, I imagined myself wearing a wedding gown. A dress that was unique yet still simple. Memorable, yet still conservative. The reception would have lots of earthy colors, and a cake made of Aggie's almond sponge.

"I should've asked you this that night at the Grizzly. I don't know what I've been waiting for."

Just say it.

I braced myself for the moment when Patrick would get down on one knee the way I'd seen men propose in the movies. His palms would be sweaty because he was nervous, and he would confess how he'd loved me since he'd moved in next door. Muffin top and all.

Patrick squeezed my hand, our fingers intertwining.

"I'm listening," I urged him on. His proposal would be the talk of the town. We would have our own spread in the *BC Gazette* by the morning—*Bison Creek Pro Falls for Timid Towny*.

"Essie, will you…" He grinned, taking a deep breath. "…be my personal trainer?"

"What?"

"My personal trainer," he repeated. "Now that I'm retired, I'll need the extra help staying in shape."

"Oh, right." I eyed Joy's bedroom door. It was now fully closed. "Yeah, of course you can train with me. In fact, Mr. Kentworth will be thrilled if it means you'll be on Pinecliffe Mountain all the time."

I shook off my wedding jitters. Very, very premature wedding jitters.

Baby steps, Essie. Baby steps.

CHAPTER TWENTY-THREE

The rest of the week had gone by as quickly as the noonday sun had disappeared behind snow clouds. Cydney had spent every night patrolling the streets, and I'd continued asking around town if anybody had seen two large Akitas called Carob and Cayenne. Sheriff Williams and Murray had managed to keep up with their usual workload while still researching Sarah Henson's journals and reviewing old evidence. But just barely.

My head had been feeling just fine, and my fingers and toes were back to their usual color. The town was preparing for the Sugar Mountain Bake-Off, and the Pinecliffe Mountain Resort was booked solid. Tourists walked along the creek near Canyon Street, ogling Lake Loxley and its solid sheets of ice. It was as if Sarah Henson's murder had happened decades ago.

Bison Creek had gone back to her daily schedule, and, it seemed, so had the killer.

"Touch anything, and I'll have you arrested." Joy glared at Wade as she counted tables and chairs. Mr. Kentworth eyed her from afar, observing his newly-appointed Head Event Coordinator at work.

"Please," Wade chided. "I can take the sheriff and his buck-toothed son any day." The resort's finest event room overlooking the ski slopes had been set up for bakers to check in with their various plates of goodies. Joy had worked nonstop all week, making sure the Sugar Mountain execs didn't regret their decision to bypass Silverwood and hold their competition in a tiny ski town that nobody had known existed until recently.

"I was talking about Essie," Joy replied with a straight face.

"Then by all means..." Wade smirked, holding his arms in the air and discreetly flexing them at the same time, "take me away." He pursed his lips, but his childish game was cut short when Joy's cheeks turned a fiery red. Wade put his arms down. "Sorry, babe."

"Go help Eli with the flower arrangements," Joy instructed him. "We all know he could use any *encouragement* to actually do his job." Wade nodded and zoomed out of the room as rapidly as he had entered.

"Will he be rewarded for that?" I mumbled.

"Not now, Essie." Joy glanced at Mr. Kentworth. He was back to his usual uptight self with his excessive spot checks and dark suits that made him look like a tall, stringy, vanilla bean. "And take Miso home before Mr. Kentworth wrings my neck for it." Joy forced a panicky smile as she looked down at her pup. "Come on, Miso."

It was Saturday morning, and for once I had some time off. But all I could do was think about the case, Patrick's *non*-proposal, and the fact that I'd been stuck with no new leads for days. Time was passing, and I was starting to hope that the murderer would reveal himself, or herself, somehow.

I held tightly to Miso's leash and strolled into the crisp morning air. I saw the shops on Canyon Street from the resort's parking lot, and Miso wagged his tail as the two of us went for a walk—a route similar to the one Sarah Henson had taken with her two Akitas every morning.

The Bison Creek Bakery was open, and Ada was inside at the counter filling a platter next to the register with scones. The windows at Doc Henry's medical office were dark. He was probably at home making his wild plum cobbler. Stella's corner market was open, as were a few other storefronts. I continued walking, stopping when I saw a large woman with a cherry red handbag trying the door to Mrs. Tankle's bookshop.

"Clementine?" I said straight away. Forcing her way inside was not the best first impression to make with a woman like Mrs. Tankle. She never forgot anything. Sometimes she still went on about how Stella Binsby borrowed her thimble thirty years ago and never returned it.

"Essie, there you are."

Her southern accent was easier to spot when she wasn't around the Jayes. Miso sniffed her shoes. High heels that had proven to be a difficult choice of footwear for the current climate.

"Mrs. Tankle doesn't open her shop until she's had her breakfast, morning coffee, and morning prayers with Bing."

"Bing," Clementine repeated. "And I thought my name was pushing it."

"Bing is her cat," I responded.

"Oh, dearie." Clementine covered her mouth, giggling as discreetly as she could. "Actually, I was looking for you. Patrick said you lived above the bookstore."

"Yes, up there." I pointed to the side of the building where a snowy staircase wound up to my front door.

"That makes sense." She huffed, pausing to catch her breath. "Here. I wanted to give you this, and let you know that I'll be waiting at the entrance with a fresh batch of Mississippi Mud Bites. I've convinced Annie Mae to come out with me this afternoon for some cocktails and some samplin.'" She pulled a piece of paper from her purse—an application and Anne's secret recipe.

"My sister said she'd sneak it into the stack, but—"

"No *buts*, darlin.'" Clementine squeezed her hands into fists, brushing her fingers across the back of each hand. "I want Anne to be pleasantly surprised when she sees how popular her desserts are." She retrieved a small bottle of lotion from her purse and rubbed it into her hands. "The air here is so dry. I'm going to run out of moisturizer in a couple days."

"Try one of the souvenir shops," I suggested. "Most of them have soaps and lotions and things like that."

"Oh, nonsense, I make them myself." She adjusted the strap on her handbag and bent down to pet Miso. "What an adorable pooch. What's his name?"

"Miso," I answered. "Don't ask me why. My sister named him."

"I've never tried miso before," Clementine admitted.

"I've never drunk sweet tea, so I guess we're even."

"How about banana puddin'?" She placed a hand on her hip.

"Maybe as a child," I confessed. "That's not something people make around here, either."

"Well then, there's a first time for everything."

Out of the corner of my eye, a shadow glided behind the door of the Painted Deer Bookshop. My blood soared through my veins, letting a shot of adrenaline kick in as I jumped back. Miso barked, but the mysterious shadow revealed itself as soon as the door to the bookshop opened. Mrs. Tankle was already dressed and ready for the day. She glanced curiously at me and my visitor.

"Mrs. Tankle," I breathed. "How long have you been in there?"

"I own the shop, Essie," she reminded. "I'm always here."

"Clementine, this is Mrs. Tankle, my landlady."

"It's nice to meet you." Rather than reaching out to shake hands, Clementine went straight for a hug. Mrs. Tankle was taken by surprise. "I'm Clementine. I'm Patrick Jaye's aunt."

"Oh, Anne's little sister." Mrs. Tankle opened the door wider, letting in gusts of winter wind that made the quilts she'd hung on the walls sway from side to side. "This is certainly a treat. Won't you come in?"

"That's kind of you," Clementine responded, "but I should be going."

"How long are you in town for? You must come to my book club next week and meet all the ladies." Mrs. Tankle studied her odd choice of footwear, and her eyes fixated on the showy color of her handbag.

"I'll be here for quite a while, actually." Clementine smoothed a lock of her dark curls. Another blast of wind blew a whiff of her floral perfume into my face. "I've decided to open a bed and breakfast. It's been a lifelong dream of mine. It's become sort of a family project."

"A bed and breakfast?" Mrs. Tankle narrowed her eyes and glanced at me. "Mr. Kentworth won't be happy to hear that, will he?"

"Some healthy competition never hurt anybody, and there's plenty of customers to go around." Clementine remained optimistic.

"Excellent point." Mrs. Tankle pointed her finger toward the resort. "I never liked the Kentworth's anyway. Drier than a burnt piece of toast, all of them. Sock it to him, I say!"

"*Mrs. Tankle!*" I blurted out, half scolding and half laughing.

"What?" She shrugged. "I may be old, but I still have opinions. Same as anyone else in this town. Whereabouts are you planning to build the place?"

"We're renovating a darling Victorian. The old Weston home."

"No!" she gasped. "You're joking." Mrs. Tankle took a step back into her shop. Her eyes darted up and down the street as if she were expecting unwanted company.

"I know it needs fixin,' but—"

"That place needs more than fixing," Mrs. Tankle responded in almost a whisper. "I'm no believer in magic or any of that hocus pocus, but that place brings nothing but bad luck."

I took a deep breath and tried to stop myself from shaking my head in disapproval. Mrs. Tankle was a believer. As someone who regularly invited her dead husband round for tea, I would say that she was *definitely* a believer.

"Are you saying it's haunted?" Clementine eagerly asked. "That would be perfect for the brochure. I tried to do a ghost tour once in New Orleans, but it was completely booked. People love that stuff."

"Keep that smile on your face," Mrs. Tankle advised her. "You're going to need it."

CHAPTER TWENTY-FOUR

The smell of sweets dominated the room so much that I thought the air might turn into powdered sugar. My stomach growled as I pushed through crowds of onlookers scattered throughout the hallway. It was time for the bake-off to begin. And as I searched the crowd for Clementine, the judges were preparing to make their rounds to sample each sweet. The judges would then vote for their favorite recipes, and the winner would be announced by the Sugar Mountain representatives.

The press was everywhere, but this time the staff knew what to do. We'd all learned our lessons last time around after Mr. Kentworth had launched a full-scale investigation as to who had let slip that the paintings in the Aspen room, the sunniest sitting room in the hotel, were all fakes. A dishwasher had been let go.

I brushed past a woman in a bright and bulky sweater bearing a picture of a cat on the front. Mim Duvall, co-owner of Bone Appétit Pet Grooming, was front and center, holding a sign with a picture of a dog eating a birthday cake that said *Sweets should be shared!* She held it up for the press to see whenever Mr. Kentworth turned his head. She attracted puzzled stares from the majority of people except Ada Adley from the bakery, who had thought it more appropriate to give Mim a high-five for her efforts.

"Essie." I turned around to see Joy jogging at an improbable speed in her high heels like she normally did—an Olympic sport she'd win if one had existed. "I'm about to have a panic attack. Can you help me line everyone up so the judges can have some space to taste everything?"

"Sure."

"Excuse me," Joy shouted over the chatter. "Hey!" She pressed her thumb and pointer finger to her lips and whistled loud enough to force a brief silence. "Everyone, please back up and wait in line!" I assisted her in guiding each participant in the right direction.

"At least Silverwood would've been more organized," I heard someone mutter.

Tables lined the walls of the event room, and the view from the window was gorgeous. Pinecliffe Mountain had just received a fresh dusting and the slopes looked smooth and powdery. The treetops were dusted as well, and the sun was finally beginning to peek through the clouds. Rays of sunshine lit the snowflakes outside like twinkling lights. With the added smell of baked goods in the air, it felt like the holidays had arrived again.

A line of people extended out of the room and into the hotel's upstairs hallway. I waved at Doc Henry, who was chatting with Booney of the *BC Gazette*, and at Stella Binsby, who was stuck in the middle of Mrs. Tankle's book club buddies. Martha Millbreck smiled and nodded at everyone who passed, but her husband was mysteriously missing from the crowd. I continued organizing the chaos, watching Eli jog past me with a folding chair. I glanced over my shoulder and saw Clementine holding tight to her sister's waist. The two of them took their place in line, and Anne gratefully accepted the chair to sit and wait in.

"Mrs. Jaye," I greeted her. "I'm glad you could make it."

"Someone wouldn't shut her mouth about it," Anne replied, nudging her sister. Clementine winked at me, and she was still wearing the same high heels I'd seen her in earlier.

"It's good to get out, Annie Mae. The fresh air will do you good."

"I haven't smelled anything like this since we took the kids to that pecan factory when they were little toddlers." She took long breaths, almost like she was struggling to take in enough oxygen. "Do you remember that, Clementine?"

"Pecan fudge, pecan brittle," she responded, gently licking her lips. "Not to mention sandies, tassies, and turtles. How could I forget?"

"I went straight home that day and made my first ever batch of Louisiana pralines," Anne declared. She paused to regain her thoughts. "And poor little Patrick had also wet himself, and needed a change of clothes."

"Definitely remember that," Clementine chimed in.

"Will we get to taste everything?" Anne asked, glancing up at me.

"I think so." I smiled. "Don't get carried away, you two." Clementine chuckled as I continued on down the line, making sure everyone was lined up properly.

Sudden clapping erupted from the front as an unfamiliar voice sounded through the speakers. A member of the Sugar Mountain marketing team introduced himself as well as his team of colleagues. The judges began eying each table, one by one, while carrying clipboards. Flossie pranced from sweet to sweet—her black-striped tights catching the attention of Doc Henry. He rolled his eyes, but his eyes fixated on her expression as she approached his wild plum cobbler.

When the judges finished making their rounds, each person in line was allowed to peruse the sweet tables in very small groups. A Sugar Mountain product table had been set up front and center, and it showed off the latest in their new line of powder blue baking dishes.

I took a turn observing the many cakes, pies, and pastries. Ada Adley had practically set up camp near her vegan oatmeal cookies so that she could inform each sampler of exactly what they were tasting—non-dairy cookies—a baking phenomenon, as she'd put it. When I passed the entry from Aggie Korston, the resort's head baker, I knew it immediately. She'd made the very cakes that had gotten me into so much trouble last month—Pinecliffe Delights. A chocolate logo of the hotel had been placed on top of each chocolate cupcake.

"Mr. Kentworth made me do it," Aggie muttered, strolling up behind me. "I so wanted to win, too."

"You still have a chance." I studied the cupcakes that were left. Quite a few people seemed to have taken some. "Though I have to be honest, those things should come with a warning."

"I told Mr. Kentworth that entering those particular sweets might've been a bit too inappropriate given recent events, but he insisted." She pressed her lips together. Her Pinecliffe Delights were amazingly chocolaty with a smooth peanut butter filling. It tasted like a fancy peanut butter cup, but in the center was a deadly surprise to anyone with a nut allergy.

"I guess taking it easy is a foreign concept to him," I agreed, noticing that much like my sister, Mr. Kentworth had not stopped working since his little hospital visit. Plus, his eyes shifted around the room like he was having trouble concentrating. *Too much coffee.*

"Or sleep," Aggie added. She forced a half-smile as an elderly gentleman in suspenders nodded with approval upon tasting one of her signature sweets. Aggie was usually uptight, and extremely bothered when everyday affairs kept her out of the kitchen. Eli had even passed by more than once and she hadn't cringed at the sight of him.

"How's that lavender balm working out for you?" I asked.

"It's like magic." She sniffed her wrist. "You try it." Aggie held her sturdy wrist up to my nose, and immediately I caught a slight whiff of lavender. I didn't understand how smelling an herb could ease the burden of having to work long hours with irritating coworkers. My remedy for that was a brisk jog, or snowshoeing up to one of the abandoned miners' cabins on Pinecliffe Mountain.

"Mmm," I lied.

Aggie raised her eyebrows as if to say, "I told you so."

I studied the rest of the entries, stopping when I came to an empty plate with hardly a crumb left. I grinned when I saw the label. Anne's Mississippi Mud Bites were already gone. She'd be thrilled to learn that the entire town had relished her family recipe. At least, I hoped she would be thrilled.

"Essie," a voice called through the crowd. "Essie!"

I narrowed my eyes as Wade approached me with a look of distress on his face. His hair was flat on one side liked he'd been dozing on the couch, and he dragged Miso's leash alongside him.

"Wade?"

"I'm glad I caught you in time." He bent down to catch his breath.

"Is everything okay?" I asked. "Is it Joy? Where is she, and why is Miso here?" I searched the room for my boss. "Wade, Miso cannot be in here right now or—"

"Sorry." Wade panted some more. "Something's come up. A slight emergency."

I never knew whether to call an ambulance or look the other way when Wade uttered the word *emergency*. An emergency to him was a lack of beer in the fridge or an empty toilet paper roll. Wade was a prime example of the boyfriend who cried wolf. But still, I racked my brain with worst-case scenarios as I waited to hear if today was finally the day he meant what he said.

"Is it serious?" I responded, glancing down at Miso, who was now tapping his nose against my leg.

"An old friend of mine needs my help." He handed me Miso's leash.

"Uh-huh."

"And Miso's been asking for a walk or whatever." He ran his fingers through his messy hair.

"*That's* the emergency?" My chest tightened, and all at once my head felt like it was in a fiery hearth. I gripped Miso's leash so tightly my knuckles went white, but Wade didn't seem to catch on to my body language. If my sister didn't kill him for being *Wade*, I just might.

"Thanks, home girl." He grinned, taking a few steps backward. "You know, I would've felt guilty just leaving him at home when it's obvious he's got cabin fever."

"Props to you for being a man," I sarcastically replied.

"You should probably drink a glass of water or something because you're looking a little flushed." He nodded as he took yet another step away from his only responsibility for the day—watching the dog that he'd adopted.

"You are aware that if you'd just bought a crate when my sister asked you to, that you wouldn't even be here right now," I added.

"Right." He chuckled. "I'm always missing something, aren't I?" He shook it off like it was no big deal. "Thanks, sis."

I clenched my jaw and looked down at Miso.

"Don't worry, pup," I said out loud. "It's not your fault."

But Miso wasn't paying me any attention. He stared across the room, his stance stiff. A low growl rumbled from the back of his throat, and before I knew it he was baring his teeth.

Miso had spotted the killer, and it was possible that the killer had also spotted him.

CHAPTER TWENTY-FIVE

My body temperature would've rivaled the Sahara's, but my brain was frozen in time.

I briefly touched the bump on the back of my head, an injury I'd sustained the last time Miso had acted this way. It was almost as if he were a different dog. His tail wasn't wagging happily, and he wasn't cozying up to any stranger who paid him attention. Miso had found his prey, and he badly wanted to go hunting.

Miso leaned forward, putting tension on his leash.

I couldn't let go or he'd fight his way through the room, knocking over tables as he went. He was strong for a dog of his size, and I did my best to stay calm. My eyes darted down his line of vision, flashbacks of Lake Loxley and Sarah Henson's frozen corpse haunting my memories.

My eyes locked with a suspect's.

Mim seemed to be the only person in the room who had noticed Miso. At first, a warm smile had crossed her face. *Someone for her to talk to.* But it didn't take long for her to realize that Miso's teeth were sharp enough to puncture skin. I held a stare equal to Miso's.

No, she can't be....

As soon as she could push her way to the entrance, Mim darted as far away from me as she could without falling flat on her face.

She is. Mim's the murderer.

Miso yanked his leash, barking loud enough to cause concern. I gulped, hoping that rushing out of the event room wasn't a mistake. A few onlookers gasped as I did my best to lead him as far away as possible without running into Mr. Kentworth. I had his leash in a death grip.

But despite all my strength training, I just wasn't strong enough.

Miso growled even louder. He took a step back and then pulled his leash so suddenly that it slipped through my fingers. I let out a yelp, feeling the coarse material clash with my palms. I had no idea a dog leash could give someone a rope burn.

I have to find Mim.

"Essie!" Patrick was at the top of the stairs holding a bouquet of wildflowers.

"Patrick?" My voice was shaky. I couldn't think straight. Miso had run off like a savage beast looking for a kill, and I was terrified at what Mim might do to silence him. "What…?"

"My aunt told me what you did for my mom." He held up the bouquet—a mixture of blues and purples. "I came to rave about her entry. That's if she isn't disqualified." He adjusted the strap of his sling and inched closer to me. "What's going on?"

"Call the sheriff," I breathed. "Call him and tell him it was Mim all along!" My feet wouldn't allow me to stand still any longer. I began my pursuit with nothing to defend myself but luck and my bare hands. I sprinted through the hotel—shiny wood floors and wallpapered halls. I listened for the sound of Miso barking, and I came to a halt. *He's downstairs.*

I sprinted back the way I'd come, pumping my arms as quickly as they would move. I passed the bake-off and ran down the main staircase, skipping steps as I went. I stopped at the second level of the hotel—rooms with less spectacular views than those on the top level. My insides jumped when I saw Mim Duvall standing all alone. She shook her frizzy hair and hardly noticed me as I ran at her.

I wasted no time tackling her to the ground—the least I could do to return the favor for when she'd tried to whack me upside the head and leave me in the snow to freeze. My breath was knocked out of me as I hit the floor, Mim crying out underneath me.

"Get off of me!" Mim squirmed, attempting to break free from my hold, but I'd clutched her wrists with an ironclad grip. I rolled her on her stomach the same way I'd squatted and lifted old man Simpkins' tractor tires for a workout. "Essie, you're insane!"

"*I'm* insane?" I retorted. "You murdered a member of our community, and *I'm* insane?"

"I'm sorry!" Mim sniffled. "She ran right into the road, I didn't even see her. I'm so, so sorry!" Mim jerked her head from side to side like she was being immersed in a giant dunk tank.

"Huh?"

"Just do it," she cried. "I deserve to die for what I did."

I loosened my grip, my chest pounding.

"Mim!" I shouted over her sobbing. "Mim, stop crying."

"I can't!" She sniffled again, attempting to wipe her tears on her sleeve, but I had her firmly secured on the ground. I shook my head. I didn't know why Mim would've wanted someone like Sarah Henson dead. Unless she'd done it for the dogs. I scanned the hallway.

"Where's Miso?"

"He ran off that way." Mim tilted her head toward the opposite end of the hallway. With more than one row of rooms on each floor and employee access points throughout the entire resort, Miso could've been anywhere.

I studied Mim's arms and legs. No bites. Not even a drop of blood.

"He didn't bite you?"

"Of course not," she argued, her dramatic cries fading away as quickly as they'd started. "Why would he bite me? Dogs love me."

"But the growling." I gulped just thinking about it. I'd come to trust Miso, but maybe he'd led me astray this time. Maybe there had been a squirrel at the window, and I just hadn't seen it. I pictured the room upstairs, searching my thoughts for a missing clue. *Too many people.*

"What are you talking about?" Mim glanced up at me like I was wearing a wig the color of Clementine's tangerine party skirt.

"What are *you* talking about?" I asked her. Mim took a deep breath as another tear rolled down her cheek.

"Mrs. Tankle's old cat," she confessed. "I ran over her last summer, and buried her in my yard."

My stomach churned, and I immediately stood up. Mim slowly rose to her feet, rubbing the red marks on her wrists. She glared at my biceps as if they'd tortured her into madness. But Mim was already teetering on the side of crazy.

"Ugh, Mim."

"I know," she blurted out. "I know I'm a fraud. A liar. A cat-killer."

"It was an accident," I reminded her.

"I should see Pastor Tad," she said quietly.

"Is that all you want to confess to?" The hotel swirled around me in a whirling dust cloud. I focused on Mim and her vacant expression. She wiped her eyes, breathing a sigh of relief as if confessing her secret to me was just what she'd needed to move on with her day. "You had nothing to do with Sarah Henson's murder?"

"You're barking nuts, Essie!" Mim scratched her head. "Barking nuts."

I rolled my eyes, continuing my search of the second level. The more I ran, the quieter the hotel seemed. The majority of guests were upstairs nibbling on cookies and fruit tarts. The second floor seemed like a ghost town. Abandoned. Silent. Creepy.

The door to a hotel room farther down the hallway opened. I stopped, waiting for its occupant to stroll into the corridor with a friendly smile.

No one did.

My feet felt like blocks of ice as I walked closer. Time seemed like it had slowed down just for me, and my thoughts started to buzz out of control. A voice inside my head cautioned me to turn around. My hands shook lightly as the memories of the shootout on the slopes last month began their instant replay through my brain.

A lump formed in my throat. I forced myself to breathe, but breathing proved difficult. My hands in tight fists, I turned to glance inside the hotel room that had seemed to float me an open invitation to investigate. A muffled bark let me know I'd tracked the right scent for once.

I stepped through the doorway, and faced the person who had *really* tried to kill me.

CHAPTER TWENTY-SIX

"I could've posted a sign on my forehead, and you still wouldn't have figured it out."

The murderer stared at me, smirking. He had one hand clamped around Miso's muzzle, and his boot was planted firmly on his tail.

"I don't understand," I said quietly. *Humor him, Essie. Buy as much time as you can.*

"Who were you expecting?" He laughed, showing the chip on his tooth that had earned him his nickname. "At least now I can finally finish the job I started."

Chip had a firm hold on Miso. He looked confident, unusually bronzed skin and all, like he'd done this sort of thing many times before. His eyes were wide, but I couldn't make out the whites in them. I ground my teeth, coming to the realization that I was officially a Bison Creeker at heart.

I hate Silverwood.

"Let Miso go," I said right away. My order came out shaky at first, but I quickly forced myself to mimic Chip's odd aura of superiority. It must be a Silverwood thing.

"And let him gnaw my leg off?" he responded. "No thank you."

My eyes darted around the hotel room. The bed had been made, but the comforter was wrinkled as if someone had been lying on it. The door to the bathroom was cracked, and a jacket had been tossed on the dresser. The remotes to the television weren't in their usual places, and a shiny token of one of Sarah Henson's accomplishments sat on the nightstand. Chip had been living here.

Chip obviously had a plan of some sort, and I needed to figure out what that was before I ended up as a block of ice in Lake Loxley. My heart pounded, and a burning filled my chest as bursts of adrenaline soared through my veins. I had little time left to act. I thought of Cydney and the pistol he kept on his hip. He'd be prepared if he were here right now.

Turn the tables. Surprise him.

"And here I thought you had a talent with animals," I muttered. Chip narrowed his eyes.

"Excuse me," he retorted, straightening his shoulders. "I have several trophies that would show exactly that." His response sparked a fuse.

"Ones with *your* name on them?" I asked, studying the tall, shiny trophy in the corner—the only one missing from Sarah's safe. The murder weapon.

"All sorts." Chip glared at me as he replied.

"Sure, but not like the ones Sarah Henson had." I took a slight step back. If I could get him to confess, and then take off running, Chip would most likely chase me through the hotel. At least, I hoped he would.

"Don't even get me started on that, cupcake." His face turned crimson, almost like I'd lit a fire in his belly. That must be his vice. Winning.

"As far as I'm concerned, Sarah and her dogs were a great success. I've seen all the trophies she kept in her closet."

"You think those dinky awards mean something?" Chip laughed again, but it was forced. He bit the inside of his cheek and adjusted his grip around Miso's mouth. All he had to do was ease up a little, and I knew Miso could break free. He'd proven to be strangely strong for his size. Or maybe he was just a fireball of gusto wrapped up in one small, furry package.

"Don't they?" I asked. Chip paused, as though taking a second to collect his thoughts. "What happened, Chip? What's the real reason you came to Bison Creek? I don't buy the whole *part owner of a pet grooming business* garbage."

"Now that is the question of the day, isn't it?" Chip's eyes darted first to the trophy he'd placed on his nightstand, and then to the armchair next to the window. "Why don't you sit down and we'll have a nice little chat about it?"

"If I sit, you let Miso go."

"Heartwarming." Chip smirked. "But I'm afraid that luck is not on your side this time."

"Why keep the dog here?" I continued. "He'll only put up a fuss. You know that."

Miso whined, but the sound of his cries only added to Chip's arrogance. He held his head proudly, pleased with himself for managing to capture me and my dog in one fell swoop.

"Leverage," he replied.

"If I cooperate, there will be no need for leverage." I scanned the hotel room for something I could use. A heavy paperweight. A piece of furniture. Anything.

The only thing that might've saved me had been used to bash Sarah's head. I shuddered as the trophy gleamed in the light. It was like a siren calling out to weary fishermen at sea. Once you got a good look at it, it was hard to concentrate on anything else.

"*If* you cooperate," he commented.

I gulped, and glanced at Miso in the eyes. There was always a chance that he would dash straight for the sheriff and bring him to my rescue. I clung to that hope as I slowly walked forward and inched myself down into the decorative armchair that matched the drapes above the window. *This might be the dumbest thing I've ever done.*

As soon as I was situated, Chip tossed Miso out the door and promptly slammed it shut. Miso barked ferociously on the other side, but Chip didn't pay much attention. He had already clamped his fist around his new toy. A shiny metal trinket that put me in an even bigger bind.

"Now what?" I said quietly.

"The things people do for their dogs." Chip rolled his eyes. "I swear if Mim were starving to death and had the choice between dog food or actual food, she would choose to feed the dogs. And probably die happy, the fruitcake." His boots thudded as he took heavy steps around the room.

"Let me guess," I responded. "You are more of a cat person?"

"Witty until the end." Chip chuckled, aiming his gun in my direction. My chest tightened as I glared down the barrel at my nemesis. "I like it."

"No, because a cat person wouldn't bother walking two Akitas in the dead of night to keep them in shape." I eyed his snow boots, the very shoes that had made footprints on Canyon Street near my apartment.

"That was clever of you to only walk them when it was snowing so your tracks couldn't be seen."

"Those two like their routine," he admitted. "Sarah spoiled them. She walked them the same route every morning. It was hard to keep them away once they got out."

"Listen, Chip." I leaned forward and casually placed my elbows on my knees. It was the only way I could think to finally suck the truth from his lips. I had to know why he did it. And I had to figure it out before it was too late. It took everything I had to keep a calm, level-headed expression on my face. I concentrated, working my way through the frustration the way I did when I lifted heavy weights in the gym. I had to ignore the turmoil going on inside, the voices that told me I was too weak, or that I would never reach my goal. "I realize that my minutes are numbered here so why don't you grant this poor girl one last dying wish?" *What did I just say?*

"You kill me, Essie." A twisted smirk graced Chip's face as he peered through the peephole. Miso had stopped barking, which meant that the two of us were finally alone.

"Why did you kill Sarah?" I focused on Chip while the rest of the room went blurry. I dug my nails into the arms of my chair. I was too anxious to wait any longer for an answer, and Chip knew it.

"First of all, Sarah isn't her real name, and I did her and everyone else in this town a favor," he confessed. "She was a troll trapped in a woman's body. A real snot."

"So you knew her well?" I shifted uncomfortably in my seat, but I stopped suddenly when

Chip took a step closer. His gun was still raised, and his cheeks were flushed, though combined with layers of fake tanner, his cheeks had turned a dark orangey color.

"Of course I did. We were both regulars on the southern dog show circuit, and good friends, or so I thought. I'm the one who suggested she breed Akitas, for Pete's sake. Do you have any idea how much Carob and Cayenne are worth?"

"The price of murder?" I guessed.

"You never quit, do you?" He took a few steps back toward the peephole. "Consistency is important when training dogs. When your pooch doesn't know what to expect, that's when the anxiety and the bad behavior shine through." His eye twitched when he spoke, and he glanced again at the trophy next to his bed.

"I'm curious," I blurted out. "What was it that brought out the bad in *you*?"

"I guess I have you to thank for that, Essie. Word is you're the one who spared this town's reputation and put it in the media's good graces. If Bison Creek hadn't ended up on the nightly news this year, I would've never noticed that footage of Canyon Street with Sarah walking her dogs in the background. We'd been living in neighboring towns all along, and we didn't even know it."

"Why did Sarah change her name when she moved to Bison Creek?" I asked. "Was that because of you?"

Chip cleared his throat, aiming his gun at my chest. His bold gesture was enough to take my breath away. I struggled to hide my nerves. My arms became jittery, and my legs felt glued to my seat like a pair of wobbly breadsticks.

"I think we're finished here, Essie."

CHAPTER TWENTY-SEVEN

I was staring death in the face yet again, and only one thought ran through my mind.

Silverwood sucks.

I cringed when Chip tilted his head. I expected the sharp sting of a bullet to tear through my body, but nothing happened. Chip raised his eyebrows. His mouth was open as if he'd just spoken to me.

"Hello!" he exclaimed. "What's with you Bison Creekers? Can't you hear properly?"

"I can usually hear myself scream," I pointed out. "Shall I give it a try?"

"You do and I shoot." Chip cleared his throat, eyeing the door to his hotel room. "Now, stand up and do as I say. Keep your hands where I can see them."

I raised my hands and slowly walked toward the door. Chip dashed across the room and grabbed his beloved trophy. He then took his place behind me, pressing the edge of his gun against my back. My palms were sweaty, but I was finally able to calm my jitters enough to think. As soon as the chance presented itself, I had to run.

"Now what?" I said quietly, stopping in the doorway. Chip glanced up and down the hallway. There was no sign of anyone, or any furry canine either.

"You and I are going for a walk." Chip nudged me forward. "Staff stairway."

Without a hint from me, Chip lightly pushed me in the direction of the staff staircase, a path that was not only the least traveled, but was also a direct route to the back entrance of the hotel. A place that was awfully close to Chip's playground of horror—the creek leading to Lake Loxley.

"My, my, you've done your homework," I muttered, pushing open the door to the stairwell. It too was empty. Chip had picked the perfect moment to reel me in. The entire hotel, staff and guests, were upstairs feasting on the cornucopia of sweets that had been brought from all over the county. And I was pretty sure Eli was up there filling his pockets with spare goods as we spoke.

"It's the eyes that lead people astray." He chuckled. "I'm smarter than I look. Smart enough to win best in show three years in a row. Well, it would have been three years if Sarah hadn't accused me of cheating."

"They say the eyes are the windows to the soul," I replied. I stepped down the first step, inching myself slightly toward the railing. Out of the corner of my eye, Chip's snow boots came into view. He stepped down, leading with his left leg. I took another step, and watched Chip do the same. He led with his left leg a second time.

"What does that tell you about me?" Chip joked, referring to my comment. I glanced over my shoulder. Chip looked down at his feet, and led with his left leg a third time.

"The road to Hell is pretty lumpy," I replied.

I flexed the muscles in my abdomen.

Just like Cydney, Chip's knees didn't always work exactly right.

And just like Cydney, Chip seemed to have a tough time with stairs.

I clenched my hands into fists, and every muscle in my body prepared itself for impact. I was about to try something that could either save me or…do quite the opposite. But I had no other choice. I lowered myself onto the next step. The end of our first flight was fast approaching.

Chip followed suit behind me, letting his good knee lead the way. His precious trophy was snugly tucked in his armpit. Mustering what courage I had, I looked over my shoulder. Just as he had before, Chip briefly glanced down at his feet. *Now!*

In an instant, I turned sideways and dropped into a plank position on one single stair. I'd done this move several times in the gym, sometimes with a pushup, but I'd never attempted it on a staircase before. I focused on keeping my core as solid as possible in order to keep my balance.

My arms collided with Chip's leg. He yelled as he struggled to find his balance, but my sudden move had caught him by surprise. He bent forward with nowhere to rest his hands but the steps below me. The hard thud of his body rolling down the staircase echoed through the stairwell. I carefully rose to my feet, observing the end result of my experiment.

I breathed a sigh of relief as I skipped down the next flight of stairs, passing Chip as he still clutched his gun and trophy while struggling to recover from his painful fall. He rubbed his head, cursing as he felt for the nearest handrail.

I reached for the door leading to the main level, but the loud bang of a gunshot forced my hand to recoil like a shaken snake. Surprisingly, in the time I had sprinted my way to safety, Chip had risen to his feet. He cursed some more as he waddled the rest of the way downstairs, his gun in one hand and Sarah's trophy in the other.

"Essie, don't you move!"

But he was too late. I yanked open the door to the staff hallway and ran as fast as I could. Another loud bang behind me made me wince. The deafening sound of his gun blasted clear through my eardrums, leaving me petrified. *Keep going. Just keep running.*

I ignored his commands, scanning the hallway for any sign of life.

Someone.

Someone must have heard that shot.

A heavy crash resonated behind me as Chip burst through the main level door in pursuit. I had no time. I darted for the exit leading to the parking lot outside. All I could do now was hope the sheriff was nearby, and that Miso would lead him to me the same way he'd brought Joy to me when I'd been left unconscious in the snow.

The cold greeted me like a hug from an awkward relative. My eyes went wide as I searched for a blanket of powder to run through. Black ice was everywhere this time of year and it was harder to spot than Mayor Millbreck at one of Pastor Tad's sermons.

My feet carried me forward as I scanned my surroundings for somewhere to hide. I glanced over my shoulder just as the back door flew open. Chip aimed his gun straight ahead of him. A trail of scarlet oozed from a cut on his forehead and trickled down his face like beads of sweat. His eyes went fiery when he spotted me. Another bang from his pistol pierced the sky, but I crouched down, rolling into the nearest pile of snow.

I brushed snowflakes from my clothes and kept moving forward. My eyes fixated on a patch of aspens in the distance. They were frosted like the peaks of the Rockies, and the surrounding brush was enough to keep me hidden. The cold tore into my lungs, and my legs felt like they'd been tossed into a furnace. I gasped, letting myself recover as I hid in a small cluster of woods near Canyon Street.

My thoughts slowed down, and so did my breathing.

The burning in my legs felt worse.

One leg, in particular.

I studied the back of my jeans.

The fabric against my calf was moist.

I'd been shot.

CHAPTER TWENTY-EIGHT

"Sarah hid too," Chip called out as he slowly studied every rock and tree. He wasn't far from me, and I crouched into the snow, hoping he'd been wrong in saying that he was smarter than he looked. "That didn't work for her, as you know."

Chip was so determined to succeed in killing me this time that he didn't even bother to wipe the blood from his face. Along with flushed cheeks, he looked more and more like a cherry-headed monster as he came into view. I gulped, taking a few steps deeper into the woods. My calf stung, and I had to cover my mouth to keep myself from groaning. I didn't know how long I'd be able to last out here.

"This never would have happened if you and your dog had just stayed out of my business," Chip went on. "You know, let me walk the mongrels in peace?" He cleared his throat and stopped suddenly. He aimed his gun and quickly shot at a nearby tree. Scraps of its trunk flew through the air.

"I know what you're thinking," Chip continued. He resumed walking forward. "Carob and Cayenne aren't even your dogs." He did his best to imitate me by lightening the tone of his voice to sound more feminine. In any other situation it would've been amusing. "That's a load of BS. Those Akitas should've been mine in the first place, just like this trophy. It was the least she could've done to pay me back for all the trouble she'd caused."

I remembered the collection of trophies in Sarah Henson's safe, including the empty space which I now knew belonged to the trophy Chip had been hoarding. Chip must have forced Sarah to open her safe and give him the trophy that was, in his mind, rightfully his. The trophy that he now clung to like it was made of pure gold. Chip must have been the mystery guest that Mayor Millbreck had heard the day he broke into Sarah's house to steal those journal pages.

Chip stopped suddenly again, rolling his eyes as he shot at another tree—this time closer to me. I took a few more steps as the shot rang through the winter breeze, putting as much distance between me and Sarah Henson's lumpy-eyed killer as possible.

"Ha!" Chip let out a hideous cackle as he stared at a familiar sight in the distance. "How convenient." Straight ahead was the frozen shore of Lake Loxley. I hadn't noticed that I'd been running straight for it, but really I'd just been looking for a good hiding spot.

I took a deep breath, working through Sarah Henson's deadly puzzle in my head. She had moved to Bison Creek a decade ago, married the first man she'd met, changed her name, and made a deal with a devil who called himself Herald. She'd slowly turned from a busybody into a power-hungry spy, recording every secret she'd learned on paper, to use to her own advantage. It made me wonder who she might've targeted next if the mayor had actually bent to her will, and had stepped down as the mayor of Bison Creek.

Making enemies must have been Sarah's thing because she'd made one heck of an enemy in Chip, a man she'd known in her past life. Apparently, she'd pissed him off so much that he'd taken the time to exact his revenge all these years later. But that still didn't explain why he'd stolen her dogs or where he'd been keeping them. If he had let them go or left them in their kennels at their owner's house, Miso would never have picked up their scent on both of those late nights on Canyon Street. He would have never followed them. He would have never spotted Chip, and I wouldn't be here cowering behind a boulder with a bullet in my leg.

Come on, Miso. Where are you?

"Let me put you out of your misery, Essie. I know solving cases can be difficult. Especially when you get it wrong." Chip took a few steps forward, forcing his legs to trudge further toward the snowy bank of Lake Loxley. "Show yourself so we can get this over with."

"Drop your gun," I called out. My stomach churned. I moved behind a neighboring tree just as Chip shot in my direction.

"Ah-ha," he exclaimed. "So you *are* disappointed in yourself for failing miserably?"

I cleared my throat. I couldn't hide forever. With every inch I scooted and slid through the woods, I was closer to Lake Loxley. Eventually my only option would be to take my chances running across the surface to the nearest refuge and hope that Chip fell through the ice as he chased me. "Don't you want to know what happened? I'll make you a little deal. You come out of the trees, and I promise not to shoot you until you've realized where you went wrong. Do we have a deal?"

He's a lunatic.

"Start from the beginning," I shouted, automatically moving to my next safe spot. A chunk of bark zoomed past me as Chip fired another shot.

"You're as stubborn as your spaniel," he commented, his eyes stopping on a cluster of trees right next to me. He took a step closer, keeping his gun held high like he was hunting wild game. I was the deer, and it was clear that Chip wouldn't stop until he'd mounted my head on his wall. "Fine." He sidestepped his way closer to me, another drop of scarlet rolling down his cheek. "Sarah and I were friends once, and we both owned show dogs that were worth a pretty penny. One day Sarah told me she'd been invited to be a judge at an upcoming show, and I was thrilled for her, of course. I knew that having an ally in the judges' corner would help me get that third best-in-show trophy I'd been working toward. But Sarah betrayed me." He paused, clenching his jaw as if the day of his defeat had been yesterday. He tightened the grip on Sarah's trophy. "She accused me of cheating, and I was banned from the competition. Worse than that, she divulged *all* my tricks of the trade right down to the fact that I'd been putting chalk in my dogs' coats to make them appear whiter."

"Chalk?" I blurted out. My heart pounded as I slid closer to the lake and farther away from my tormentor. Only a handful of trees separated us.

"She single-handedly tanked my business," Chip stated as another droplet of blood oozed down his face. The streaks of crimson were quickly becoming a prominent facial feature. "We're talking hundreds of thousands of dollars down the toilet, and to top that all off, one of Sarah's show dogs won best in show the following year. That lying wench cheated me, and then cheated herself in order to win. I called her out on it on many occasions."

But then she moved away.

"I warned her that I'd get even," Chip continued with his story. "But before I could gather enough evidence to ruin her reputation, she took off. I assume that's when she settled here, bought herself a couple of Akitas, and started meddling in *other* people's lives."

"So you killed her for a trophy?" I asked. My chest tightened, and a sharp pain seared up the back of my calf. I clutched it tightly, hoping that too much blood hadn't soaked into my pants. A crunching noise rang out in front of me. Chip was only steps away, and I wasn't ready to die.

"Hey, I gave her a chance to make things right. It was fate that a cousin of mine lives in Silverwood. I moved there to start over with a fresh breed of pups. As soon as I saw Sarah on the news, I convinced Mim to give me a piece of her store in exchange for more business. It was too easy." The sound of his voice sent chills up my spine. He was close enough to me that he didn't need to shout. "I watched Sarah. I even followed her, but she caught on quick. So, I went to her house and I confronted her."

"You made her give you that trophy." I gulped.

"She gave me what was mine in the first place, but then she ran." Chip chuckled, glancing off into the distance like he was watching that night play out on a movie screen. He smirked. "She said I'd never get away with it. That she was a force to be reckoned with in this town, and I just better *watch my step*. I showed her."

"That's quite a confession," I commented, scooting back through the snow. I was too late. Chip finally stepped through the trees, holding his gun level with my head. Sarah's trophy sparkled in his opposite hand. I stared up at him. His sinister eyes were wide with excitement, like a savage beast was lurking behind them. He wasn't sorry for what he'd done. Not one bit.

"I jammed her beloved trophy into the back of her head," Chip whispered. "Mother Nature took care of the rest. Let that be a lesson to you, Essie. Never step on someone else to get ahead. It comes back to bite you in the end."

He pursed his lips together, twitching his trigger finger.

"Wait!" I blurted out. I was at his mercy until I could muster the strength to stand and fight back—my last and only option. "You haven't told me what I did wrong."

"*Everything.*" He laughed. "You asked about my eye condition, and I told you the name of it. A simple online search would've revealed that I've spent a little too much time where the sun shines like fire." He shook his head as if he was disappointed that I'd bothered asking him the question. I squeezed my calf and cautiously rose to my feet. My leg throbbed—an intense storm of pain that shot up my back. "Where is Sarah from? *Dallas, Texas.* The state listed on her pathetic collection of dog show trophies? *Also Texas.* The answer was practically branded on my face. Plus, I'm from Silverwood. I was expecting the sheriff to bust down my door. But no."

"I'll keep that in mind next time," I said under my breath. My leg was cramping up. My body was in agony from the tips of my icy fingers to the bump on the back of my head. I had to at least *try* to make it out alive.

"I don't think so," Chip muttered through his teeth. He tapped his finger on the trigger of his gun, reminding me that he was in charge.

A bark called out in the distance, giving me the extra ounce of spunk I needed to wrestle Chip to the cold, rocky ground. My eyes settled on his stupid trophy as I searched my brain for ideas. Anything that might help me overpower a man who was bigger than me.

I doubt he's faster…or lighter. Definitely not lighter.

Another bark in the distance came to my rescue, and Chip made the mistake of turning his head to see how close my four-legged menace had come to sniffing him out. He grimaced—a face similar to that of the misbehaving dogs he groomed at Mim's shop.

I leapt forward like I was jumping into the deep end of a swimming pool. My arms hugged the trophy that Chip had so fervently carried with him all this way. He was attached to it. More so than he was to anything else because he immediately concentrated all of his efforts into forcing me to let go of his prized treasure.

"Ah!" Chip yelped as he fell backwards, yanking the trophy out of my hands, but dropping it himself in the process. His back hit the icy ground with a loud thud, and the sound of growling next to him was like music to my ears. Miso bared his teeth the same way he'd done many times before. He snarled and went for Chip's forearm like it was an old dog bone. Chip squealed and let go of his gun. Sarah's trophy rested in a patch of snow in between us.

"Essie!" a voice called for me, and I paused to take a breath. I limped toward the gun and quickly tossed it into the woods behind me.

I had done it.

I'd solved another case, and I was still alive.

I breathed in the cool mountain air and let it brush against my rosy cheeks. Chip groaned at my feet. Now that he'd confessed, Cydney would take care of the rest. It was what he loved, his favorite part of detective work. Following protocol.

A hand clawed at the wound in my calf, and I couldn't help but scream. Pain surged up and down my spine with an unforgiving sting. I fell to my knees, and that was just what Chip wanted.

"Not so fast," he forced himself to say. His voice was raspy, and the odd color on his face made it obvious that his wounds were making him queasy. Miso licked my cheek, nudging me to stand up. "Wretched dog!"

Like Frankenstein being brought back to life, Chip forced himself to his feet.

Miso barked, signaling to my rescue team where I was. A crowd of people stood in the distance, one of them running right for us. Chip wasted no time swinging his leg back and thrusting it toward Miso. The sound of Miso whining from the cold tip of his boot made my eyes well up with tears.

Miso barked in response, and grabbed the thinner end of Sarah's trophy with his mouth. Chip's eyes went alight with revenge yet again. He wobbled forward as Miso trotted through the snow closer and closer to Lake Loxley with the trophy between his teeth.

Chip trudged past me and straight toward the frozen lake. I could make out the midnight shimmer of Miso's coat in the distance. He had no trouble maneuvering his way over cracked sheets of ice until he was as close to the center of the lake as he could be without falling into the icy waters beneath. *Please, don't fall through. Please, don't fall through.* Miso dropped the trophy onto the ice and came trotting back to shore.

Chip cursed some more as he fought to keep his balance. He placed a foot on the thick sheet of ice at the shoreline. He was going to go after his trophy. Like a pirate after his stolen wares, he was determined to claim his rightful property.

"Chip!" I shouted. I did my best to follow him. I glanced down at my shoes, and concentrated on my stride. Each step I took felt like murder. I stopped when I reached the edge of Lake Loxley.

"Stop!" I yelled. Chip continued onward as Miso scurried past him and back to dry ground. He stopped at my side and wagged his tail.

"Hey, you there!" Cydney was right behind me. "Stop! Put your hands in the air!"

Chip didn't care; it was almost as if he hadn't heard Cydney's warning.

"Chip, you'll fall through!" I warned him, but Chip was hell-bent on getting his hands on the trophy he'd envied for a decade. Even if that meant it was the last thing he'd do.

Oh, snowballs.

"What in the world is he doing?" Cydney muttered. His gun was drawn, and his eyes observed every inch of me for injuries. He narrowed his eyes when he spotted the back of my calf. "Essie, you should get yourself back to the hotel."

"I will." I watched Chip walk closer and closer toward the middle of the lake where the ice was thin enough to crack to pieces. Falling through this time of year would be fatal—a severe shock to the system that would be sure to take his breath away and never give it back.

"Is he crazy?"

"What do you think?" I said, answering his question with a question. Cydney rolled his eyes. It was nice to have some normality back in my life. Having a gun pointed at me had reminded me how much I took the average things in my life for granted. A warm apartment. A fluffy pillow. A dead car.

"I order you to stop!" Cydney shrugged, gun raised.

Chip glanced over his shoulder before making one last break for the trophy. He ran forward, but the ice did the rest for him. He fell to his knees, and then to his stomach, and slid farther away from the shore.

I scratched Miso behind the ears as a crowd of gawking tourists formed behind us. Bursts of chatter broke out around the lake as more and more people pointed and gasped at the lunatic that was continuously slipping in the distance. Some whispered, and some spoke plainly. Cydney turned around, shaking his head.

"What the blazes?" Sheriff Williams mumbled, finally catching up. Murray trailed behind him.

"I told him to stop," Cydney told him. "I can't help that he's a fool."

"He's after one of Sarah's trophies," I clarified. "The murder weapon."

"So, he's—"

"Yes, sir," I said, adding, "he told me everything."

The sheriff nodded.

"Essie, why are you still here?" Cydney scolded me. He pointed to my gunshot wound, and I realized the spot on my calf was starting to feel numb.

"Scoot on over to Doc Henry before I write you a ticket," the sheriff insisted.

Miso barked, pulling my attention back toward the lake. A wave of gasps traveled through the crowd—now both townies and tourists—at the shoreline. Chip was just feet from his prize. When he finally brushed his fingers against it, he held it in an ironclad grip and raised it in the air. He'd risked his life for a stupid object. A false confidence-booster.

Sheriff Williams stood steadfast, waiting to make an arrest as soon as Chip was within reach. Chip studied the crowd gathering near the shore, and instead headed in the opposite direction—an area of Lake Loxley that almost definitely wouldn't hold his weight. Chip held tight to his trophy, glancing back at all of us with a twisted smirk on his face.

Miso barked again.

Chip took pride in his steps as if he'd outsmarted the entire town. Maybe he had. But he'd also outsmarted himself. As sure as he'd been warned, the surface of Lake Loxley started to crack, but Chip sojourned on.

Crack.

Chip slipped.

Crack.

The surface beneath him separated.

Crack.

"Oh, have mercy!" a woman gasped as Chip disappeared into the wintry water below.

In his thirst for revenge, he too had met the same icy fate as Sarah Henson.

CHAPTER TWENTY-NINE

"How does that saying go?" Joy was standing beside my hospital bed picking through a box of assorted chocolates. It was one gift of many. Word had spread through town that I'd been the one who uncovered the truth, and of course Doc Henry had confirmed that my efforts had come with a price this time. A shot to the leg.

"If you're going to eat that caramel, just eat it," I responded. "Don't take a bite and put it back."

"What if I don't like it?" Joy took a taste of another chocolate and tilted her head as she chewed. "That's an entire piece of chocolate wasted."

"That's what the pictures on the box are for."

"Revenge is a dish best served *cold*," Joy declared, pointing her finger in the air as if the saying had just come to her. "Ironic, isn't it?" She glanced down at the chocolate box, avoiding looking me in the eyes. Instead, she tapped her fingers on the table next to my bed. My room was plain white, and yet it was comforting to be able to rest my head knowing that the real murderer was gone. Now, I could finally sleep.

"You didn't come here to tell jokes and sample all my presents," I commented. Joy took a deep breath and set the chocolates down. She crossed her arms.

"What makes you say that?"

"They're letting me go in a couple of hours," I answered. "Besides, you haven't told me who won the bake-off. It was front page news before the…incident. You have something else on your mind."

"Why is it that you got all the smarts?" she teased, but teasing was her way of easing the tension. I knew that because I did it too. Sometimes too much.

"I'm the adopted one, remember? So that's a discussion for another day." I cleared my throat, glancing around the room. I'd never expected to be back in this place so soon.

"Wade and I found a place," Joy admitted. "I was going to tell you after the bake-off." She clasped her hands together. Her fingers were long and thin, much like her. She was taller than me, and the closer she came to my bedside the more she towered over me like she used to when we were kids.

"Congratulations," I responded. "I hope you'll invest in a thick pair of curtains."

"Wade knows the rules." Joy chuckled. "No nudity when company is around."

"Let me know how that one goes."

"So, you're not mad?" She paused, watching my expression for any hint of frustration.

"Don't be silly."

Joy hadn't stood in the way of my relationship so I couldn't stand in the way of hers. Besides, if history had taught me anything, Joy would be back to being my roommate in a month—tops. Unless she was right, and things between she and her ex really were different this time around.

"Good," Joy went on, "because there's something else." She bit the corner of her lip, unsure how to proceed. "You know how I'm really horrible at admitting when I'm wrong?"

"Like *now*, for example?"

"I was wrong," Joy confessed. "I'm not maternal at all. I don't think I was made that way."

"You want me to take Miso?" I guessed. Joy nodded. The thought had crossed my mind many times. For some reason Miso trusted me, and now I trusted him completely. He'd saved my life. "I guess in a weird way I knew that was coming."

"Or we could look for a new family for him," Joy continued. "I didn't know looking after a dog would be so hard. And no one tells you that they follow you around *everywhere*."

"No," I replied. "I think he's already found his family."

Joy smiled, a sincere smile that lit up the rest of her face and erased the look of annoyance that was normally glued there instead. A light knock on the door interrupted us, and I sat up straight as Patrick entered the room. I smoothed the bottom half of my hospital gown and quickly ran my fingers through my hair.

"Joy, good to see you." Patrick lifted his elbow then winced, forgetting that he was wearing his sling. "I don't think I'll ever get used to this thing."

"Patrick." Joy raised her eyebrows, her eyes darting from him to me. "I'll see you back at the apartment, Essie."

Joy left the room in a flash.

"Oh." I sighed. "She forgot to tell me who won the bake-off."

"My money was on the Mississippi Mud Bites," Patrick responded. He casually glanced at the monitors near my head. Most of them were off. Patrick's hazel eyes wandered to the bandages on my leg. "But sadly,

Mom did not win. Though she was asked several times for her recipe. It was a big crowd-pleaser. It cheered her right up."

"Good. That was the point."

"The prize went to Betsy from the hair salon for her Full Moon Whoopie Pies. The judges said, and I quote, that they were 'out of this world delicious.'" He shrugged as best he could.

"And you agree?"

"I wouldn't know," he responded. "I didn't taste them. I was too busy following a little black and white spaniel around the hotel." He grinned, pulling me back to the last moment our eyes had met.

"I see." I took a deep breath.

"Any chance that little dog can come over and sniff around my new place?" His eyes were gleaming as he awaited my answer.

"You mean, sniff around for bad guys?" I joked.

"Something like that."

"I was wondering when you'd invite me over," I continued. The more we talked, the easier it was to be myself around him. My old self—the quiet girl from next door with a sharper than average tongue.

"Technically you're not invited," he retorted. "Just Miso."

"I see." I cracked a smile.

"Please don't tell me you already have plans for the week."

Up until now Patrick and I had spent little time together since his wedding fiasco last month. I knew that he wanted to move on with his life as much as I did. And he wanted to spend it with me. It still seemed like it was yesterday that the pair of us were building snow forts in the backyard until our fingers turned raw. It was like nothing had changed, but I knew better than to actually believe that.

"I think I can squeeze you into my double life."

"Right." Patrick's jaw protruded. It was his filler motion, much like the way some people twiddled their thumbs or cracked their knuckles. And some just uttered the word *um*. "Part fitness trainer, part…"

"Police assistant?" I said. "I'm still working on a better title than town consultant."

"How likely are you to end up here next time?" His hand reached for mine.

"I don't know," I answered. "But I promise you that the Bison Creek hype will eventually die down. Well, hopefully not too much. One hospital stay is good enough for me."

"Except this time it was *two* hospital visits," he pointed out. Our fingers intertwined, and he gently squeezed my hand as if our limbs were carrying on their own conversation. I squeezed back, my heart drumming.

"This won't happen again."

"You don't know that for sure," Patrick replied.

"True, but I do know that I'm not ready to leave the station just yet. I think I can make a difference there, and Sheriff Williams isn't the grouch that people make him out to be."

"If it makes you happy." Patrick leaned in closer, ending his sentence with a kiss. Immediately, my cheeks felt warm and my chest tingled. Now that the case was off my plate, I had time to think about my next big hurdle.

Taking my relationship with Patrick to the next level.

And there was also a chance that he would be the death of me one day, according to Flossie.

* * *

"I believe in magic," Murray recited with a smirk on his face. "I really do, Pop." He sat forward in his chair holding his evening coffee as Carob and Cayenne pranced around the station with Miso at their heels. Miso's midnight coat contrasted with the light fluffiness of Sarah Henson's two Akitas. After searching Chip's hotel room, Cydney had found a receipt for a storage unit just outside of town. Sarah's dogs were found there, in their kennels with plenty of food and water.

As soon as I'd been released from the hospital I went back to work, spending some of my afternoons at the station sorting through complaints. Some had been legit, but most were residents calling to complain about yappy dogs and snow that needed shoveling. The majority of these came from old man Simpkins, a former school principal who hated children.

"I'm sorry, how is this relevant?" Cydney was standing next to the sheriff with a pile of Sarah Henson's journals at his feet.

"I just thought you boys should know." The sheriff paused. "And Essie." He rubbed a piece of his smooth mustache. *Maybe he does that for good luck?* "As of today I am no longer a smoker." Carob, the dominant dog of the three, stopped and barked. Sheriff Williams jumped, slightly startled and still not used to having two bear-like canines strutting around his place of work. "We *really* need to find a suitable home for those two."

"Are you finally quitting because of what Mom said about—"

"Shush." The sheriff held out a hand, silencing his son. "I have decided to stop smoking for health reasons."

"*Obvious* health reasons," I muttered. Murray glanced at me and grinned. He held up his coffee mug as if toasting to my comment.

"As I was saying." Sheriff Williams cleared his throat. "I've tried the patch, the gum, and all those things in the past but they never worked. I've been meeting with Flossie, and she has me drinking all kinds of juices and whatnot. Anyway, it seems to be working this time."

"I support you on this new adventure of yours, Sheriff," I commented, knowing full well how hard it was to give up a habit like his. I still wrestled with my conscience every morning when I smelled Joy's first brew of the day. I missed the caffeine, but I didn't miss the crashes and the headaches from one too many cups. We all had vices that taunted us.

"I appreciate it, Essie." He exhaled loudly as he reached into his shirt pocket. It was empty. "I feel naked without my smokes, though."

"Keep a pack of gum in there for a while," I suggested. The sheriff shrugged, considering the idea.

"Well, shall we?" Sheriff Williams said, gesturing toward the nearest exit.

The four of us gathered Sarah Henson's journals and carried them out back, where Murray had prepared a tall trash can to burn them in. We'd agreed to destroy them as soon as the investigation had ended. The information written throughout the pages was enough to send the townsfolk on a wild rampage. Not to mention, the things contained in each book could have been deadly in the wrong hands. For once, we'd all agreed to kill that possibility before it had the chance to come back and haunt us. Those books couldn't be known to exist if Bison Creek were to remain a quiet mountain town.

Sheriff Williams tossed the last of the journals into the can, along with the mayor's missing pages, and nodded at Murray to douse them in lighter fluid. A flame rose high, ridding us of ten years of intrusive spying. Cydney looked away, having lost his argument with the sheriff about the policies on destroying evidence even if it was from a closed case. But in the end, he had understood.

"I was never here," Cydney mumbled, shaking his head.

The smoke rode the winter wind like an ocean wave, and I stared at the firelight. The ashes would give Bison Creek a clean slate, and I was one hundred percent ready to leave Sarah Henson's murder case behind me. Carob, Cayenne, and Miso played together in the snow. Carob and Cayenne seemed especially thrilled to roll around in the fresh mountain powder.

"Any word from the Millbrecks yet?" I said quietly, taking a step toward Cydney.

"They're taking a time-out to work on their marriage. Conveniently, this little time-out just so happens to be in the Bahamas." He crossed his arms, disappointed. After the fiasco at the lake, Mayor

Millbreck and his wife had left town for an extended holiday. They'd assumed that their secrets would be leaked around town, and they didn't want to stick around and watch. Maybe Bison Creek would finally have a new mayor.

"Everything will work out fine," I insisted. "Maybe Herald will do the right thing and step down."

"I highly doubt that. The Millbrecks aren't known for owning up to their mistakes."

"And speaking of mistakes," I added, "it seems that I owe you an apology." He raised his eyebrows. "Don't get too big-headed, okay? I just wanted to say that I might've misjudged you. When we first met I thought you were an arrogant, uptight know-it-all who wasn't right for this town."

"I see." Cydney chuckled, puffing out his chest. "And now you think differently of me?"

"No," I answered, glaring at the way he straightened his shoulders just to make himself that much taller than me. His attempts to assert his dominance were about as pointless as Cayenne's. "I still think you're all those things. *But* maybe you are right for this town after all."

"*And?*" Cydney paused and studied my expression. Like a true detective, he tried to sniff out the root of my compliment.

"What better way to fit in with the locals than to become the proud new father of a couple of fur balls?" I blurted out.

"Ugh." He rolled his eyes. "I don't do hair on the furniture and slobber everywhere. If you're so concerned, why don't you take them?"

"You've met my landlady, right?"

Our arguing continued until the flames in front of us started to die down. I called Miso, and he happily obeyed. The two of us said our goodbyes and strolled down Canyon Street, heading for home. Snowflakes danced up and down our path, and the street lamps in the distance made the snow glow. A crisp breeze brought a smile to my face.

Everything was as it should be.

Miso pulled at the leash.

I glanced up the street, and my heart pounded as a stray cat popped out of nowhere and crossed our path. I forced a nervous smile, but the faint jingle of its collar was a familiar sound. The sound that Patrick's childhood cat, Snowflake, used to make when she wanted to be let inside. Now, Patrick claimed that Snowflake was his guardian angel cat, still roaming the streets of Bison Creek warning him of any dangers that lay ahead.

I wasn't superstitious like Patrick was, but I couldn't help but wonder if the cat was a sign. I squinted, trying to make out the jagged shape of the tag around the cat's neck. Strangely, it did look like a snowflake. I quickly walked toward it, but just as fast as it had appeared in the middle of the road, the cat was gone.

Good ol' Snowflake.

EPILOGUE

It was a book that easily blended in with the rest, but each page had been handwritten. Being the sheriff of Bison Creek, Ronald Williams had never meant to break the law, but yesterday was an exception. It had to be. Otherwise, a lifetime of secrecy would have all been in vain. Sheriff Williams slid the leather-bound journal toward his wife, Sharla. She placed her hand on it, and a tear gleamed in the corner of her eye as if she was absorbing all the sorrow from its pages.

"Are you certain that *no one* saw you take this?"

"As far as the others are concerned, this journal burned with the rest of them," the sheriff replied.

"What about the new detective?" Sharla questioned him further. "Are you sure he can be trusted?"

"He hasn't spoken out of line as of yet. He's young. I don't think he'll be a problem."

The sheriff stroked his mustache, a smooth patch of facial hair that he'd had since he'd first taken the position of sheriff, employing his son to work alongside him—a failed attempt at building a better relationship with his offspring than Ronald had endured with his own father.

"What about Essie?" Sharla anxiously awaited the opinion of her husband. "I told you to stay away from her, but—"

"I've pushed her out of my life for long enough," Sheriff Williams responded.

"She's a smart girl, Ronald. It's unwise of you to form a relationship with her."

"She *won't* find out," the sheriff reassured his wife. Since Essie Stratter had started assisting him in his inquiries, the storm clouds over the station had disappeared. The folks of Bison Creek didn't run the other way when they saw him coming. Stella Binsby didn't give him the evil eye on his morning walk to the bakery. Murray was always in a chipper mood, and he had started combing his hair more often.

"Let's hope so." Sharla, on the other hand, was not so convinced that the changes at the station would end in applause. She was more concerned about the consequences of playing with fire.

"Maybe things don't have to be this way," the sheriff suggested. "Maybe all these changes are fate's way of making things right again."

"*Fate?*" A light knock on the door announced an overdue visitor, who flew into the conversation as if she were riding on a broomstick. "You believe in *fate* now, Ronald? That's laughable."

"It's about time you joined us, Florence." The sheriff eyed a woman who, in his opinion, wore too much black and had no business buying fishnet stockings at her age.

"Have you smoked today?" The woman, named Florence but better known around town as Flossie, observed the overall energy that seeped from her client's aura. Contrary to the old saying to never judge a book by its cover, Florence believed that first impressions told her everything she needed to know about a person.

"Of course not," the sheriff answered. He was determined to quit for good this time, especially after Doc Henry had called him two days ago with some not-so-friendly test results.

Florence looked to Sharla.

"He's telling the truth," Sharla confirmed.

"Well, bravo." Florence took deep breaths, avoiding the one thing in the room she could not have predicted. The contents of the late Sarah Henson's diary.

"Did you warn her like we discussed?" the sheriff asked.

"Yes, I did." Florence recalled sitting at a far-off table at the Bison Creek Bakery. "I pretended to read her palm and then I told her."

"Did she believe you?" The sheriff had been set on finding a way of interfering without actually interfering. This had been the best way he could think of.

"I don't know, Ronald." Florence shook her head. Essie was a particularly hard person to read. Being quieter than most, she kept her true thoughts locked away in her head. "I mean, I can't even read palms so I don't know how convincing I sounded."

"So what do we do now?" Sharla asked.

"We *watch*, and we *wait*." Sheriff Williams clasped his hands tightly, hiding his fears from the others. "There's still a chance that everything will remain exactly as it is."

"Oh, don't kid yourself," Florence responded. "I thought we fixed this mess a long time ago."

Sharla nervously opened the journal in front of her and flipped through its pages. She stopped when she reached the particular entry that had made her husband suspicious. So suspicious that he'd spent all night at the station reading every last word that the late Sarah Henson had written. Luckily, Sarah had had no idea what she was seeing at the time.

"Apparently not," Sharla answered.

Recipes

ANNE'S MISSISSIPPI MUD BITES
A sweet southern treat!

CHOCOLATE SQUARES
1 cup (2 sticks) unsalted butter
2 cups sugar
4 eggs
2 teaspoons vanilla extract
1/2 cup unsweetened cocoa powder
1 1/2 cup all-purpose flour
1/4 teaspoon salt
1 cup pecans, chopped
1 cup chocolate chips
3 cups mini marshmallows

CHOCOLATE FROSTING
1/2 cup (1 stick) unsalted butter, softened
6 tablespoons unsweetened cocoa powder
3 cups powdered sugar
1/4 cup milk

NOTE: This dessert is very rich, and best served in
bite-size squares after sitting in the fridge overnight.

In a large mixing bowl, cream together the butter and
sugar. Add the eggs, and vanilla extract, and mix well.
In a separate bowl, sift together the flour, cocoa
powder, and salt. Add the dry mixture to the butter

mixture, and mix until it forms a chocolate batter. Stir in the pecans and chocolate chips.

Pour batter into a large, greased casserole dish (9x13), and bake at 350 degrees Fahrenheit for 35 – 40 minutes, or until a toothpick comes out clean. Place the mini marshmallow on top, and bake for an additional 3 – 5 minutes. Let the dish cool completely before frosting.

For the chocolate frosting, whisk together the butter, and half of the powdered sugar. Add the cocoa powder, milk, and the rest of the powdered sugar, and mix until smooth. Gently frost over the melted, cooled marshmallows, and set the dish in the fridge for at least 30 minutes. Cut into small squares, and serve.

CHOCOLATE BANANA ICE CREAM WITH NO-BAKE BROWNIE BALLS

Essie's go-to comfort food

CHOCOLATE BANANA ICE CREAM
3 bananas, sliced and frozen
2 tablespoons unsweetened cocoa powder
1 – 2 tablespoons cold water (as needed)

BROWNIE BALLS
9 -10 pitted dates, soaked in water
1 cup raw almonds
1/4 cup unsweetened cocoa powder

For the brownie balls, soak the pitted dates in water, and set aside. In a blender or food processor, grind the almonds to make almond meal. Add the cocoa powder, and dates. Blend until the mixture forms a chocolate dough. Use a tablespoon to scoop the dough into round balls, and place in the fridge for 10-20 minutes. This recipe makes about 12 brownie balls.

For the ice cream, use a blender or food processor to combine the frozen bananas and cocoa powder. Blend until the mixture resembles frozen yogurt. Add additional water (only if needed) to help the ice cream blend completely. Scoop into a bowl, add the brownie balls, and serve immediately. This recipe makes about two servings.

ADA'S VEGAN OATMEAL COOKIES
Too good to tell the difference

2 cups oats
1/2 cup sugar
1/2 teaspoon ground cinnamon
1 teaspoon baking soda
1/2 cup cashew nut butter
1 teaspoon vanilla extract
1 cup raisins, soaked in water

NOTE: Be sure to save the water used to soak the raisins. This recipe requires 1/2 cup of the soaking water.

Pour the raisins into a bowl, and fill to the top with water. Set the raisins aside to soak. Using a blender or a food processor, grind 1 1/2 cups of oats into oat flour, and set aside. In a large mixing bowl, combine the oat flour, sugar, cinnamon, and baking soda. Add the cashew nut butter, and vanilla extract, and mix well. Add the remaining 1/2 cup of whole oats, raisins, and 1/2 cup of the water the raisins were soaked in. Mix to form cookie dough. Use a tablespoon to scoop the dough onto a greased baking sheet. This recipe makes about 24 cookies.

Bake at 350 degrees Fahrenheit for 15-20 minutes, and let the cookies cool before serving.

Books by A. GARDNER

Bison Creek Mysteries:
Powdered Murder

Iced Spy

Frosted Bait

A Flurry of Lies

Southern Psychic Sisters Mysteries

Dead and Butter

Mississippi Blood Cake

Dead Velvet Cheesecake

Lemon Meringue Die

Chocolate Dead Pudding

Pineapple Upside Drown Cake

Poppy Peters Mysteries:

Southern Peach Pie And A Dead Guy

French Macarons And A Dead Groom

Bananas Foster And A Dead Mobster

Strawberry Tartlets And A Dead Starlet

Wedding Soufflé And A Dead Valet

To learn more about A. Gardner, visit her online at:
www.gardnerbooks.com

Made in the USA
Middletown, DE
14 November 2021